P9-AFL-137

"No, I haven't changed my mind"

Jud's eyes were icy cold as he went on: "Are you saying that you have? That your mother's ring doesn't mean as much to you as you thought?"

There was ice in his voice, too, and Lucy had the definite conviction that no one had ever before gone back on a deal with Jud Hemming.

"And if you have been thinking of changing your mind, forget it! You agreed to be engaged to me for three months—you'll go through with it right to the very last day."

Lucy's voice was almost as cold as his as she flung the words at him. "I've never gone back on my word in my life!" But fear struck through her knowing that whatever happened in the months ahead, there would be no avoiding Jud's unnerving presence!

OTHER
Harlequin Romances
by JESSICA STEELE

Hostile Engagement

by

JESSICA STEELE

Harlequin Books

TORONTO·LONDON·NEW YORK·AMSTERDAM
SYDNEY·HAMBURG·PARIS·STOCKHOLM

Original hardcover edition published in 1979
by Mills & Boon Limited

ISBN 0-373-02302-2

Harlequin edition published December 1979

CHAPTER ONE

LUCY looked away, keeping her features impassive. She had seen the look that man had sent her way many times before. To give him his due his glance hadn't been as obvious as some of the 'You and I could make sweet music together' looks she had previously received, but it had been there, she was sure of it.

She had learned how to deal with such glances, had learned not to give encouragement when she had no intention of playing the game through to its ultimate end. She had been avoiding such glances ever since the promise of beauty had broken through before she had left her teens behind. But there was something about the man, she had no idea what; he didn't look very different from anyone else in the room, but something about him had her by now veiled eyes returning to him.

He wasn't looking at her—and that surprised her slightly because having expected him to seize on the opportunity to catch her eye and move on to the next surface gambit of the smile, the edging over to where she was to introduce himself, she saw that he was in conversation with an elegantly turned out older woman, a blonde girl about her own age, and Joyce Appleby, the only person in the group she knew. Lucy turned her attention away from him and listened to what Philippa Browne at the side of her was saying.

'Is your brother here?' Pippa asked. 'When I spotted you I thought Rupert might be here too.'

They were at a 'Strawberries and Champagne Morning', another of Joyce Appleby's mad ideas for raising money for charity. It was being held in the village hall and Lucy had

thought the time of the venue as much as the pricey tickets
would have kept a lot of people away, but the room was
crowded, so perhaps to hold it on a Bank Holiday Monday
hadn't been such a mad idea—and on second thoughts,
Lucy reconsidered, money would be no object to any of
the people here anyway.

'Rupert couldn't make it,' Lucy told the mousy-haired
girl by her side.

'Out with that Sandra Weaver, I expect,' said Pippa,
looking downcast for a moment. I wish he was out with
Sandra, Lucy thought; she would far rather he was out
with the gay divorcee Sandra than the company he was
mixed up with at the moment. 'Oh, there's Justin Arbuthnot with his parents,' said Pippa, her spirits brightening.
For all she was the same age as herself Lucy thought Pippa
a little immature at times, her whole thinking seeming
to revolve around men. 'Will you excuse me, Lucy? I'll just
go and have a word ...'

Left by herself, Lucy took a small sip from the champagne glass in her hand. It was her first glass and she didn't
intend having another; she was only here anyway because
Rupert had insisted they must keep up appearances. She
dragged her mind away from that thought and looked
round the room. There were plenty of people she could
have gone to join, but she wasn't interested in idle chit-
chat. Having put in the appearance Rupert was so keen on
she'd just finish her drink and go home.

She felt her eyes drawn to the man whose glance she had
caught earlier and though hating not being able to resist
let her gaze rove casually round the room till they rested
on the group he was with. Joyce Appleby was still with
them and Lucy wondered, since Joyce was well known for
extending her love of humanity further than required, if
she had him lined up for her next paramour. She reckoned
Joyce would have her work cut out, for though he seemed
to be listening with interest to what Joyce was saying, Lucy

thought she detected a sign of polite tolerance on his face that otherwise looked particularly expressionless.

Not once did he glance over to where Lucy was standing, but she was convinced she had read that first look correctly—that he hadn't looked at her again meant only that his approach was different. Since he seemed now to be captivated by what Joyce was saying, Lucy felt free to give him close scrutiny. He was taller than average, but it wasn't that that made him stand out from everyone else in the room, for stand out he did. She tried to pinpoint what it was about him that had eyes other than her own on him, but she couldn't pin it down. She hadn't seen him before—perhaps he was visiting someone in the area; she paused to wonder if he was already Joyce Appleby's lover, though she couldn't quite see him in that role. He looked the sort of man who would want more from a relationship than the surface prattle Joyce could churn out unceasingly from dawn to dusk ...

Damn, she swore silently as the subject of her thoughts raised his eyes from the women around him and caught her looking at him. Hurriedly she dropped her eyes, but not before she had seen his glance pass over her without halting—without seeming to be aware that she was in the room, causing her to wonder for the first time if she had imagined that look after all. She had been so sure ...

'Hello, Lucy—haven't seen you in an age.'

Lucy turned to find Donald Bridges at her elbow, and although she'd had cause at one time to give Donald short shrift she was suddenly glad to have someone to talk to. If the man who had just looked through her as though she didn't exist flicked his glance her way once more he would know she wasn't invisible to everybody.

'Nice to see you, Donald,' she replied with more warmth than had been in her voice the last time she had seen him.

Donald's long-toothed smile was much in evidence as he beamed at the 'no hard feelings' note in her voice. 'Sorry

I got carried away the last time you came out with me, Lucy,' he apologised, the suggestion of a smile on her face giving him the courage to bring the matter out into the open. 'You're so beautiful I rather lost my head ...'

'Let's forget it, shall we?' Lucy said quickly. She knew she was letting him off lightly—he had been a veritable octopus when he'd taken her home from dinner that night, seeming to have at least four pairs of hands all going in different directions, and if there was one thing she couldn't stand, it was being pawed about by over-amorous young men.

Donald seemed as pleased as she was to let the subject drop. 'Bad do about your parents,' he said, his smile disappearing making his face solemn. 'I wanted to write to you after the accident, but I thought after the way we parted that night you wouldn't want the unpleasant reminder of me while grieving for your mother and father.'

Lucy's face was as solemn as his as she recalled the dreadful shock she and her brother had received when they had learned that their adored parents had been drowned in a sailing accident. She and Rupert had received other shocks since then, but nothing that had followed had been as great for her as that of knowing she would never see her beloved parents again.

'I didn't expect to see you here today,' Donald was going on. Half of her mind registered what he was saying and she made the correct rejoinder, she thought, but the other half of her mind was taking a line of its own as it progressed from Donald's innocent statement that he hadn't expected to see her at the charity function.

She hadn't wanted to come, had only given in to Rupert's persuasions because he was going through such a very bad time. She had got ready knowing she was going to hate every minute of it, had dressed in her silk jump suit, donning with it her own share of pride that decreed she would attend and show the people they had always considered their friends, but who Rupert had said probably wouldn't want to know them once the news was out that the Careys were penniless that the Careys were still as good as any of them. Perhaps penniless was a bit of an exaggeration, she thought, since Rupert had an allowance doled out to him quarterly under Grandfather's will—though his allowance would barely keep them ticking over. Rupert didn't come into the whole of his inheritance from Grandfather until he was thirty and he had another five years to go before he reached that age—how they were going to manage until that time was anybody's guess. Already they had parted with several good pieces of furniture, having found a mountain of unpaid bills and no money to settle them when their parents had died. There was little else to sell that wouldn't make it obvious to anyone who called at Brook House that it was not so well furnished as it had once been. Brook House was much larger than they needed, she mused, but Rupert refused to sell the house and move into something smaller. She couldn't blame him really, she supposed; the house meant the same to him as the antique ring that had been her mother's had meant to her—Lucy forced down the tears that rushed to her eyes as she recalled the day Rupert had told her he had lost it. He knew how much she valued it and it had been weeks before he had confessed that he had lost it when taking it to the jewellers to have it polished and cleaned.

Hiding the sorrow of her thoughts, Lucy realised Donald had been talking to her for some minutes and she hadn't heard a word he said; he must have been unaware she wasn't listening, but now apparently he had said something that required an answer.

'I'm sorry,' she apologised, 'with all this racket going on I missed what you were saying.' She accompanied her words with a smile just in case he saw through her lie.

'I know you'll think I've got a bit of a cheek, but I was asking if you would come out with me some time?'

Lucy looked at him and decided that with or without the change in their fortunes she wouldn't have accepted his offer anyway, for all he would know better than to come over all amorous another time—but if what Rupert said was true, that she and her brother would soon be out of this set, then for pride's sake she was glad to be in the position to turn down an invitation rather than wait for invitations to stop altogether. Coming here this morning had been a final farewell in a way to all the people she had known for so long, though none of them here would know it.

She could have left Donald's offer hanging in the air, all she had to do was say 'Give me a ring some time', but she didn't. 'I don't think so, Donald,' she said, and watched the expectant smile disappear from his face and almost weakened as she felt an unexpected sadness at that moment. Then knowing it was the way it had to be, she smiled gently, regretfully, 'Would you excuse me Donald, I told Rupert I wouldn't be too long.'

She hadn't told Rupert anything of the sort, she mused as she left Donald and went into the short hall and from there into the small cloakroom. For all it was late May it was cold outside and she had slipped a jacket over her shoulders before she left Brook House. Almost everybody there must have been feeling the cold too, she thought as she saw coats, wraps and scarves covering every available surface, the half dozen or so hooks on the coat rack over-burdened until it was impossible to hang anything else there. Lucy had just spotted part of her white bouclé wool jacket beneath a pile of others, when the blonde girl she had seen in the group with the man whose look she had mistaken came in.

'Just off?' the blonde asked, seeing Lucy endeavouring to extract the white bouclé without dropping the ones on top on to the floor. 'Not a bad do, was it?'

'Not bad,' Lucy agreed, liking the girl's open friendliness for all they hadn't got around to being introduced.

The blonde rectified that omission with the same ease she had struck up the conversation. 'I'm Carol Stanfield, by the way—I came with Jud and his mother.' She took it for granted Lucy knew who Jud and his mother were.

As she was about to introduce herself, the top coat of the pile Lucy was wrestling with began to slip, taking her mind off telling the other girl her name as she grabbed at the coat before it hit the ground. So the man who had looked through her was called Jud, she thought as she replaced the coats, deciding to tug at the flash of white and hope for the best. She doubted she would ever find out his surname—she had never seen him in Priors Channing before, so he must, she concluded, be visiting someone in the district. Quite what made her ask the question she didn't know, because she just wasn't interested in where the man lived, but as the girl who had introduced herself as Carol Stanfield saw the wrap she had come in for on the top of a pile near the door, the words left Lucy's lips before she could stop them.

'You don't come from around here, do you?'

'Lord no! I live in London—you never know, though ...' she smiled a friendly smile. 'I'm staying with Jud up at the Hall,' she said, and held up crossed fingers. 'Here's hoping,' she added impishly, and not noticing Lucy was staring at the hand, fingers now uncrossed, Carol Stanfield placed the wrap over her arm and turned to go. 'See you around, I expect,' she said, and was through the door before Lucy answered her.

All Carol Stanfield's talk and what exactly it was she was hoping for passed Lucy by. She was too stunned to do little more than realise she was now in the cloakroom by herself. That was my mother's ring, she thought, stupefied, when at last her brain began to function again. Carol Stanfield had been wearing the antique ring Rupert had lost that day he had been taking it to the jewellers in Dinton.

Galvanised into action, Lucy went to hurry after the

other girl, her jacket forgotten, it was of prime importance
to stop her before she left. But before Lucy could reach
the door the pile of coats from which Carol Stanfield had
taken her wrap slipped, and Lucy was ankle-deep in outer
garments of all colours. Unable to open the door, she had
to first pick up the jumbled heap of furs and fabrics. It
didn't take very long and with an unspoken apology to their
owners she plonked the bundled assortment on the small
table all anyhow and dashed through the door.

She reached the open front door in time to see a smooth-
looking Bentley pulling away with the blonde head of
Carol Stanfield sitting in the back. Wild visions of sprinting
to her Mini and chasing after the Bentley sprang to Lucy's
mind, only to be halted by Joyce Appleby's tinny tones.

'Ah, Lucy, just off, are you? So pleased to see you—you
didn't bring Rupert with you? He's a naughty boy—but tell
him we'll forgive him.'

Lucy had forgotten Joyce was on the organising com-
mittee. She was just the right person to do the job, she
thought, but she was more anxious to get away than to
stand listening to Joyce—she knew of more than one person
who had given a donation to one of Joyce's charities purely
in order to be rid of her.

At last Lucy made her escape and went to retrieve her
jacket and put the bundle she had tossed so unceremoni-
ously down by the door into some sort of order. It was too
much to hope that the Bentley would still be around and,
her mind busy, Lucy got into her Mini and followed the
route the genteel Bentley had taken down the road.

Carol Stanfield had said she was staying up at the Hall
with Jud. The only Hall Lucy knew of in the district was
Rockford Hall. It had been up for sale for ages, as had the
estate and farms that went with it. No one knew the exact
asking price, but common sense said it must go into seven
figures. The man Carol had called Jud must be rolling if he
had bought it, Lucy considered, and surely anyone con-

nected with him wouldn't have come by her ring by any
underhand means.

Undecided whether to make straight for the Hall or go
home with the hope that Rupert would be there—he had
gone a bit wild just lately, understandable really, she excused him with sisterly blindness—Rupert would know
what best to do. Something, she didn't know what, stopped
her from turning the Mini on to the road that would take
her to the Hall when normally there would have been no
decision to make. At any other time there would have been
no arguments. She would have sailed straight up to the
door of Rockford Hall and demanded to see the wearer of
her ring.

She didn't want to see the owner of the Hall, though.
A feeling of unease spread through her at the very thought
of seeing him and stating baldly that his guest was wearing
her most treasured possession. She had a feeling he
wouldn't like it—not that she was frightened of him, he
might well be very understanding about it, though she
wasn't very convinced about that.

Trying hard to remember on which hand the girl had
worn the ring, Lucy turned the Mini in the direction of
her home, Brook House. Had Carol Stanfield been wearing
the ring on her engagement finger? Perhaps she was this
Jud person's fiancée—that made it even blacker, for if
Carol was engaged to him, and good luck to her if she
was, she would need all the luck she could get if first im-
pressions were anything to go by—then wasn't it likely
that if the girl had grown attached to the ring she would be
most unlikely to want to give it up? Try as she might Lucy
could not remember on which hand or even which finger
the girl had worn her mother's ring. All she knew was that
it was the same ring and she wanted it back at all costs.
What was more, she was going to have it back—regardless
of whatever Jud whoever he was had to say.

Parking her car in the drive of Brook House she saw

Rupert's car was parked beside the big oak front door of the many-windowed Georgian house, and raced inside to find her brother, anxious to tell him her news.

She met Rupert coming along the hall obviously on his way out. 'How did the bunfight go?' he paused to ask.

'I saw my ring,' Lucy came back, too pent up to answer his question, and followed on in a rush, unable to see her brother's expression in the dim light of the hall. 'There was this girl there and she was wearing it, Rupe—she was wearing my ring! She ...'

'Your ring?' Rupert interrupted her slowly when she would have galloped on. 'You say you saw a girl wearing your ring?' he questioned, then to her utter amazement discounted what she had just told him. 'You must have made a mistake.'

'I didn't,' Lucy said quickly, not comprehending that Rupert didn't believe her, and went on to tell him what had happened.

'It was probably very similar—but I doubt it was the one I lost,' her brother said when he had heard her out. She wished he would come into the sitting room with her where they could discuss it in relative comfort, but Rupert hadn't moved towards the sitting room but seemed to be edging nearer to the front door if anything.

'It was the same ring,' Lucy told him flatly. 'I'd know it anywhere.'

Rupert peered at his watch. 'Look, Lucy, I know you're in a lather, but I'm supposed to be seeing Archie Proctor in ten minutes—leave it until I come home, we'll talk about it then.'

Mention of Archie Proctor successfully took her mind off the ring for a moment. Archie Proctor was one of the few friends of her brother's whom she didn't like; he was too fond of the good life without thought for the consequences for her peace of mind—there was that girl over at Bishops Waking who claimed openly that the father of her daughter was Archie Proctor, for all he denied it.

'What are you seeing him for?' She knew she shouldn't question Rupert like this, but she was never happy when he was out with Archie Proctor. Rupert had only taken up with him since their parents had died, and she fervently hoped he would drop him as quickly.

'I *am* three years older than you, remember,' Rupert came back, not liking to have his movements questioned. 'At twenty-five I think I'm entitled to make friends without having to ask your permission.'

She had upset him. She didn't need to hear the front door slam behind him to know he had taken exception to her question. Disconsolately she pushed her way into the sitting room and stared with unseeing eyes out of the window. The gardens were a picture this time of the year, but it could have been a dung heap out there for all the beauty she saw.

There was no knowing what time Rupert would be back. More than likely he and Archie would go into the nearby town of Dinton and live it up till the small hours. Once or twice lately Rupert had come back the worse for drink, though Lucy didn't know where he was getting the money from; his allowance wasn't due for some weeks yet, but that wasn't her main concern just then. All she hoped was when he came home it would be in one piece, having caused no harm to himself or anybody else.

Telling herself that worrying over Rupert wouldn't bring him home any sooner or any more sober than he would be if she didn't worry about him, Lucy went to her room and changed her jump suit for jeans and a sweater, while niggling worries of Rupert kept intruding. She had no idea what time he would be home and she so wanted to have her ring in her possession tonight. He had said they would discuss it when he came home, but as far as she could see there was nothing to discuss, even supposing Rupert was sober enough to discuss anything very sensibly.

He had been so loving and caring when their parents had been alive, immediately afterwards too, she recalled, and although grieving their parents' loss himself, had gone out of his way to help her with her pain. She brushed a tear from her eyes as she recalled the day he had seen her sitting holding her mother's ring—she had no idea of its worth, but treasured it because it had belonged to her mother; it had in fact been in the family for generations. Rupert had taken the ring from her; there had been no need to ask if she loved it, he knew that already. 'I'll take it into Dinton tomorrow and have it cleaned up for you,' he had told her gently. 'I don't suppose Mother's had it cleaned in all the years she's had it.' That he had spoken of their mother in the present tense had gone unnoticed by both of them; at that point they were still referring to their parents as if they were still with them.

True to his word Rupert had taken the ring into Dinton. But it was not until three weeks later that he confessed he had lost it, and by that time they were acquainted with, and trying to adjust to, the news that the fortune they had expected to inherit was non-existent, were adjusting to the fact that the lands to the north, east and south of Brook House had been sold off some months before to pay for their father's gambling debts, debts they had been in total ignorance about—that they still had the house was a miracle. Seeing how bitter Rupert had become at the news that his inheritance had been gambled away from him, Lucy had bottled down her anguish over the loss of her ring, and had asked her brother quietly if he had informed the police.

'Of course I've informed them,' he had snapped, none of his earlier gentleness in evidence then. 'What do you take me for—an idiot?'

'I'm sorry,' she had apologised, and kept the sorrow of her feeling to herself.

After that Rupert had shaken off the bitterness of his feelings and had replaced it with a wildness that was so out of character she began to wonder if she had ever truly known her brother at all.

Knowing she would not be able to sit quietly waiting for her brother's return, Lucy thought briefly of ringing the police and letting them handle the investigation into how Carol Stanfield came to be wearing her ring, but after some time spent in thinking the matter over, she decided against the idea. If this Jud person had just come to live in the area it was hardly fair, knowing how quickly gossip could spread in the community, to have speculation spreading about him or his guests being the receivers of stolen property—that sort of talk would take years to live down in the close community of Priors Channing, and while she held no brief for him, in all fairness she knew she couldn't do it. No, there was only one way to handle this—she would go to the Hall herself.

Once her mind was made up Lucy found it difficult to wait until she judged lunch at the Hall would be over, then at two o'clock she went to her room and exchanged her jeans and sweater for a lightweight trouser suit in mid-brown that went well with her dark brown hair and eyes; the whole effect was lifted by the cream silk blouse she donned beneath her jacket. She could have gone up to the Hall in her jeans, but the knowledge of what would almost certainly turn out to be a sticky interview ruled that no matter how she was feeling inside, she should arrive at the Hall looking cool, neat and confident, and she doubted that jeans and sweater would help her achieve that effect.

On previous visits Lucy had made to Rockford Hall, the journey from Brook House had always seemed longer, but within a very short space the Mini was turning through the wrought iron gates at the bottom of the long drive. Rockford Hall had previously been owned by Colonel Broughton, a friend of her father's. Lucy remembered trying to keep her mind away from the interview in front of her which she just knew wasn't going to be easy. When Colonel Broughton had died two years ago the whole property, including the tenanted farms that stretched as far as Bishops Waking, had been left to the Colonel's nephew Selwyn. Selwyn had never shown an interest in the Hall and when he had learned the amount of death duties he had to pay had lost no time in putting the Hall and its farms up for sale. The grounds of the Hall, neglected since the property had been empty, showed signs of someone having made a start on getting them back into shape—a mammoth task for anyone, so more than likely an army of gardeners had been taken on, Lucy reasoned, as she turned the wheel of the Mini and pulled the car to a halt by the large imposing front door.

Attempting a cool façade just in case anyone was watching from one of the windows, she left her car and sauntered up to the stone steps. That her hands felt clammy and her insides trembly she put down to the fact that if Carol Stanfield was engaged to this Jud, then she was bound to be upset at having to give up her engagement ring, and Lucy had never intentionally hurt anyone's feelings, besides which she had taken to the friendly girl who had introduced herself and then disappeared.

Lucy thought to have a few more moments in which to compose herself while waiting for her knock to be answered, but while she was still taking a deep and steadying breath the door swung inwards, and she found herself face to face with the man she had come to see. At once she recognised that expressionless face. If he was surprised to see her then his surprise wasn't showing, and she only hoped the nervousness she was suddenly feeling was not in evidence for him to witness.

'May I see you for a moment?' The words sounded remarkably cool in her own ears, and she was glad that whatever he had made of her in those first seconds, there was no hint of hesitation in her voice to betray her true feelings.

Though when he made no move to stand back and allow her to enter, she thought she was going to have to state the nature of her errand on his doorstep. 'My business won't take long,' she found herself saying into the stifling silence.

The door was opened, and without saying a word, the man she had come to see stood back to allow her over his threshold. The light in the hall was much better than at the hall of Brook House, and vaguely Lucy noted the different set of furniture from the last time she had been here when the Colonel had been in occupation, though it was not so very different in that the hall was still tastefully furnished with a smattering of antiques.

Carol Stanfield was standing at the foot of the stairs with every appearance of making for one of the upstairs rooms. Lucy calculated that she and Jud—she wished she had discovered his other name, since she could hardly call him by his first name—they must have been crossing the hall when her knock at the door had sounded and without waiting for one of his staff to answer the door he had performed that service himself. That in itself told her he was no snob.

'Hello,' said Carol Stanfield, still in the same friendly tones she had used only that morning—Lucy regretted that Carol wouldn't be feeling so friendly towards her at the end of her visit. 'How nice of you to come to see us.'

'This isn't a social call,' Jud put in at the side of Lucy, causing her to glance at him and quickly away. His expression was inscrutable, telling her nothing other than that she had definitely, but definitely, imagined that 'your place or mine' look at the village hall this morning.

'Not a social call?' Carol was obviously having a hard time wondering what on earth his visitor could want to discuss with him that wasn't social.

'I—er——' Lucy was now hating the reason for her call as she watched Carol's puzzled face.

'I'll see you later, Carol,' said Jud, indicating that Lucy

should follow him into the room she knew used to be the drawing room.

'You mean I can't come with you?' Carol queried.

That was the last thing Lucy wanted. She was going to have a hard enough time convincing this sombre man at her side that the ring was hers without the added disquiet of trying to convince him while the girl she was sure now was his fiancée was present.

'I'd rather see Mr ...' Oh God, she wished she knew his name, wished it was over. 'I'd rather see him alone.' She didn't look at him to see what he was making of it.

'Don't be long, then, Jud—you promised to teach me to play billiards, remember,' said Carol, having to accept that her presence wasn't wanted.

'This shouldn't take long.'

Lucy silently echoed his words with the fervent hope that inside ten minutes she would be driving away from Rockford Hall with her mother's ring in her possession.

The man she knew as Jud closed the door of the drawing room behind them, and looking directly at her indicated that she should take a seat on one of the several giant-sized settees the room housed. Lucy didn't want to sit down, she felt too uncomfortable in this man's presence—this man who by his very silence wasn't making it any easier for her to begin. But she felt compelled, as he stood silently waiting, to sit down, if only to give herself some small thing to do. Straight away she wished she hadn't, as he remained standing, and as she looked at him, taking in that he was taller than she remembered with him towering over her, she saw he looked ten or fifteen years older than herself, had dark hair the same as she had, but that his eyes were a hard grey-green. In fact it was not only his eyes that were hard—the whole appearance of the man was hard: hard mouth, hard muscular body.

'The name is Judson Hemming.'

His voice was just as hard as the rest of him, she thought,

as he reminded her that she had called to see him on a business matter without even knowing his name.

'I'm sorry.' She wished she hadn't apologised, it gave him the advantage straightaway. 'We never got round to being introduced this morning, did we?' That was better, her voice was sounding quite cool again. 'I'm Lucy Carey—I live at Brook House.'

He received this information without comment, and she wondered if he already knew who she was. Anyone could have told him at the village hall, though he didn't look as though he was sufficiently interested enough to enquire. She wasn't used to this sort of treatment from a man. It jolted her a little to know how indifferent this man was to her.

'You said you wanted to see me on a business matter,' he reminded her darkly, as though to suggest that if she didn't soon spit it out he would very shortly be showing her the door. 'I'll warn you now, Miss Carey, guessing games aren't much in my line.'

His sarcasm stung, making her head come up sharply, putting starch into her wilting backbone, making her so angry that sparks flew to her eyes. Judson Hemming was just about the most impossible man she had ever come into contact with. He had known from the very beginning that she was uneasy and had done absolutely nothing to spare her feelings, so why should she consider his? She had right on her side after all. She stood up and felt better that although he still topped her by a head, she was more on a level with him.

'Neither do I go in for guessing games Mr Hemming,' she retorted, striving to keep cool. 'But I thought because you're new to the district it would be better to see you first rather than follow my first inclination and go to the police.'

Again that inscrutable look was on his face—would nothing shake him? He hadn't so much as batted an eyelid at her mention of the word police, but just waited silently and watchfully for her to continue. If his face was showing anything at all, it was utter boredom.

Lucy had never been aware of boring anyone, indeed had found herself more than popular right back through her schooldays, and she wasn't going to stand for it. Her business was stated flatly and with complete disregard for any feelings he might have, since she was beginning to doubt he had any whatsoever.

'The ring your fiancée is wearing is mine,' she stated baldly, and expected another sarcastic comment as the blunt statement left her, but was shaken to see he was completely unmoved, even to the extent of ignoring her claim.

'You're engaged to be married, Miss Carey?' he queried. 'Not to the young man I saw you talking with this morning, I trust? There didn't seem to be very much joy on your part from what I could see.'

Completely taken out of her stride, Lucy looked straight into cold, hard grey-green eyes. 'I'm not engaged,' she snapped. 'Donald reminded me of something ...' she broke off abruptly. It was nothing to this man that Donald had brought everything crashing in on her memory—the sad thoughts he had unintentionally triggered off.

'Something ...?' Jud Hemming questioned. 'If the look on your face was anything to go by your memories would appear to be very sad ones, Miss Carey.'

'I'm surprised you noticed the look on my face,' she said stonily, then wished she hadn't because now he would know she had noted his indifference to her.

'I probably wouldn't have done,' he came back, unperturbed, 'other than that a solemn face stuck out like a sore thumb among so many happy smiling faces. What, I wonder, were you thinking about to make you look so sad?'

Had there been any sign of sympathy in his tone she might have clammed up, for everyone had been kind and sympathetic to her and Rupert when they had lost their parents, and the sympathy of people had made it hard for her to hold back the tears which in private had flowed unendingly. But with this man's abrasive attitude she knew she would never ever be at risk of breaking down in his company.

'My parents were drowned in a sailing accident some months ago—it was the first time I'd seen Donald for him to offer his condolences.'

Lucy looked away from her interrogator as the words left her lips. She knew what she had told him wouldn't affect him one way or the other— how could it? He hadn't known her parents, hadn't known the sweetness of her mother, or the devil-may-care man who had been her father. All the same, she was not as tough as she thought she was, and having made her revelations she felt the tug of tears behind her eyes, until Jud Hemming's abrasive tones hit her ears.

'So this Donald fellow is not a regular boy-friend?'

She answered him purely because she needed a moment or two to pull herself together. 'No—no, he isn't—nor likely to be.'

'Should one say "Poor Donald", I wonder?'

'What do you mean?' Tears were very far away suddenly as she snapped back. The way he had voiced his question led her to believe he considered any boy-friend of hers would deserve a medal.

'It's obvious the chap is keen on you. Equally obvious is the fact that you aren't too keen on him—why, I wonder?'

Conscious that this interview had not only been taken completely out of her hands, but had gone so far away from the point at issue that it looked a long road back, Lucy almost spat the words at him. 'Because I had occasion to box his ears the last time he took me out,' she snapped, and was instantly aghast that this man she barely knew had extracted that piece of information from her that normally nothing would have had her revealing. 'Look,' she went on, furious with herself now as much as him, 'can we get back to the reason for my call . . .'

'Ah yes. You are laying claim, I believe, to my—er—fiancée's engagement ring.'

'It's *my* ring,' Lucy reiterated. 'To be more precise, since you seem to want to know everything, it was left to me by my mother. It has great value to me, and *I want it back.*'

CHAPTER TWO

'So,' Jud Hemming said consideringly. 'You say the ring is yours. Which I wonder has the greater value to you—the fact that your mother left it to you, or the actual monetary value of the ring itself?'

Lucy felt sick that anyone could feel the need to ask such a question, and raised hurt eyes to his hard stare. She saw his jaw harden briefly before he grated at her:

'You think that an unfair question? Believe me, it isn't. There are plenty of women around who don't give a damn about sentiment—women whose whole slant on life is jaundiced by a materialistic outlook.'

'And you think I'm one of them?'

'I'm hardly in a position to judge, am I? Seeing that before today I had never set eyes on you.'

Lucy didn't swallow that. Jud Hemming was a type of man she had never come across before, but even so she had a shrewd idea he could look, sum up, and file away, all in the space of five seconds.

'Well, I'm not,' she said clearly. 'You seem to have been particularly unfortunate in your—er—relationships with my sex—but we each get from a relationship what we put into it, you know.' She was rather proud of her little homily. That should put him in his place, she thought, a feeling of triumph washing over her that for the first time since she had entered this room she felt on top—her triumph was shortlived.

'Is that why you felt it necessary to box this Donald chap's ears?' he asked smoothly.

'I . . .' He had her there and he knew it. She hadn't given Donald that sort of encouragement, but he had made a grab for her just the same.

'So if I'm to believe you,' Jud Hemming went on when it became apparent his remark had floored her for the moment, 'you're asking for the return of property you say is yours, not because of its financial worth, but because of the sentimental attachment you have to it?'

Lucy nodded. 'I'm not even sure of its true value in pounds and pence,' she stated, and when he raised a disbelieving eyebrow, she went on, 'Rupert—my brother—was going to get a jeweller's estimate of its value so that we could insure it. He was taking it to be polished and cleaned when he lost it.' She didn't like confessing that bit, but knew before this man would let her have her ring back he would want to know how she had lost it in the first place. 'Rupert thought it might be insured for about eight hundred pounds—only we weren't sure.'

Jud Hemming looked at her steadily for several seconds, then announced shatteringly, 'I paid three thousand for it.'

'*Three thousand—pounds?*' She wished she had never stood up. She would give anything now to have something solid supporting her. 'The ring is worth three thousand pounds?' She couldn't take it in, and she had an idea her astonishment had got through to the man who had paid out that amount without apparently turning a hair, and that he believed she really hadn't known how much it was worth.

'You had no idea, had you?' he seemed to be saying from far off. Then with an irritable movement, as though believing her when he didn't want to irritated him, he said harshly, 'Do sit down, Miss Carey—you'll make the place look untidy if you give in to your obvious desire to pass out.'

Lucy felt his hand on her arm, nothing gentle in his touch, then she was seated on the settee she had leapt up from earlier and he was handing her a drink that fired the back of her throat after the first sip. Then as her brain started to function again, she began to realise the impossibility of her task. If he had paid three thousand for the ring he wasn't likely to hand it over without kicking up a fuss about it. Refusing to be daunted, she placed the remains of her drink on the small table to the side of her. She was going to see this through to the bitter end if it killed her.

'The last thing I want to do Mr Hemming,' she said slowly, choosing her words carefully, 'is to upset Miss Stanfield, but I can only repeat what I said at the very beginning—I want my mother's ring back.'

Jud Hemming looked into the glass of Scotch he was now holding. She hadn't noticed him pouring it, so reasoned he must have decided he wanted a drink when he had poured her the brandy. Then he was looking directly at her, his cold eyes showing not a glimmer of emotion.

'And how do you propose to pay me the three thousand pounds I parted with?'

Lucy held his look for as long as she was able, but she was the first to look away as it dawned on her that somehow or other this man knew what pride had ordered that no one in Priors Channing should know until it could possibly be avoided; he knew that she and Rupert were stony broke.

'I ...' She refused to be defeated, and lifted her eyes again bravely. 'I shouldn't think it will come to that—surely when you tell the police who you bought it from, they'll be able to trace it back to whoever found and subsequently sold it in the first place.' As she followed that thought on though, Lucy realised that whoever had received Jud Hemming's money would in all likelihood by now have spent it, and there would be little chance of his money being returned to him.

If he was having the same thoughts, it didn't show in his face. But what he said precluded that the culprit would ever be brought to book. 'Ah, but you see, Miss Carey, I have no intention of telling the police or anyone else the name of the person who sold me the ring.'

'But ... but that's ridiculous! You'd be letting a criminal get away scot free—it ...' She stopped as she could see she wasn't getting through to him. He had made up his mind not to reveal the name of his—what was the word she was searching for—fence? No, that made Jud Hemming a criminal too. 'It's aiding and abetting,' she accused, bringing out a term she had heard used on television.

'Not at all—I bought that trinket in good faith.' Trinket? Three thousand pounds? Lucy swallowed an angry comment as he continued. 'I have a bill of sale, and at the time of the purchase I had every confidence that the person who sold it to me had every right to sell it.'

'And you refuse to say who that person was?' He didn't answer. She had known she was wasting her time asking the question anyway—she could see from the set of his mouth that he was determined to keep that piece of information to himself. 'So in order to reclaim my property, I shall need to tell the police that you have it?'

'That could prove a costly business,' he said silkily. 'To gain possession by those means will involve long and expensive court proceedings—I will not be forced into giving up anything that is mine.'

Lucy's heart sank. She had had a premonition this wouldn't be an easy interview. How right she was to have been nervous about coming face to face with this unbending man! There had been no need for him to underline how expensive it would prove to take him to court—she had read of cases where costs had gone into hundreds of thousands. Her eyes flicked round the room, and discreet though every piece of furniture in the room was, she could tell without putting a price tag on any of it that it had cost a fortune to furnish this room alone, and knew without question that Jud Hemming could afford to take any case she brought against him all the way. She would get cold feet at spending as much as a hundred pounds while knowing he would have one of the cleverest lawyers available working for him.

'So the only way I'm going to get my ring back is by paying you the three thousand you paid for it?' she asked, feeling weary, fed up and frustratingly angry all at the same time.

'The ring isn't for re-sale,' she was told bluntly. Then after a long moment when her spirits hit zero, he added, 'There is a way in which I will return it to you—though I'm not certain the sentimental value of your inheritance is sufficient for you to contemplate agreeing with what I have to suggest.'

'I'll do anything you ask,' she said proudly, having no idea what he had in mind, though if he wanted her to white-wash the stuccoed outside walls of the Hall she would do it, for all it would probably take her ten years, from the sheer size of it. She looked steadily back at him, intrigued to know what she could possibly do for him that warranted him handing over an item of jewellery he had paid three thousand pounds for. The very air around them seemed to be taut, and she sat silently, holding her breath as she waited. Then shakingly, shatteringly, Jud Hemming's eyes locked with hers, refusing to let her look away, and he announced with no sign of emotion in his voice at all:

'I will return the ring to you provided you wear it on your engagement finger.'

'Engagement finger ...?' she queried, her incomprehension showing in every contour of her face. She just couldn't understand what he was asking. He couldn't be saying he intended to remove the ring from Carol Stanfield's hand and that she should ...

'To be more precise, Miss Carey, I'm saying I want you to be engaged to me.'

'You're joking!' It was out before she could stop it. The tightening of his lips told her he wasn't joking, though she hadn't needed that small movement to tell her he rarely, if ever, joked in his life. He was a particularly dour man, she thought. 'But why? I ... I mean, you're already engaged to Carol Stanfield, aren't you? What's she going to say about this? She'll be dreadfully hurt.' As yet it wasn't sinking in that he was serious, even though she knew she couldn't doubt it.

'As a matter of fact I am not engaged to Carol,' he said smoothly.

'B ... but she was wearing your ring?'

'I didn't give it to her.'

'You mean she just—took it?'

He didn't answer, and Lucy's imagination took off. Light was just beginning to penetrate. She saw it all now. He had tired of his affair with Carol—Lucy didn't at that point speculate why then had he invited Carol to stay at his home —while from Carol's point of view she wanted something more permanent from him than to be just another mistress. Carol must have seen the ring—probably in his bedroom, Lucy didn't wonder—and had laid claim to it. With the unshakeable belief he had that all women were nothing more than gold-diggers that wouldn't have endeared Carol to him, and in order to extricate himself from the situation, Jud Hemming wanted to use Lucy as a means of finishing his relationship with the poor girl.

'What about Carol's feelings?' Lucy blurted out. Surely Carol would be deeply hurt if Lucy agreed to his suggestion to become his fiancée—she wanted her ring back, certainly, but she had to live with herself, didn't she? Could she be hard enough to take what was rightfully hers and in so doing cause that friendly girl so much unhappiness?

'Carol's feelings need be no concern of yours,' Jud Hemming said coolly, then with that hard note returning to his voice, 'Either you wear that ring as my fiancée, or you don't get it back—take it or leave it.' With that he turned his back on her and went over to the drinks cabinet and replenished his glass.

Lucy wasn't sure which feeling was uppermost in her mind at that moment. Anger that he could so callously get rid of the girl who at one time *must* have meant something to him rose within her. Carol couldn't have just invited herself to the Hall, she reasoned. Why, his mother was here as well, wasn't she? She had been at the village hall this morning anyway, and if Carol Stanfield had been just a passing affair she couldn't see a man like him introducing her to his mother. Anger vied with sympathy for the poor girl, who in her opinion didn't look in the least like a gold-digger, then her anger gave way to the thought that if Jud Hemming wanted to be rid of her poor Carol was going to be hurt anyway, and there was nothing Lucy Carey could do about that. That thought salved her conscience somewhat—it was her ring, after all. He had gone to stand at the other side of the long room—he had given her an ultimatum; 'Take it or leave it', he had said, and had made no attempt to persuade her to do what he wanted. Coldly, clinically, he was putting her sentimental attachment to the ring to the test. It was entirely up to her whether she took his offer or not—one thing was for sure, he wasn't going to lose any sleep whatever she decided.

'H ... how long will this engagement have to last?' she asked his back. There was no question of romantic involvement—she shuddered at the thought; it was expedient at the moment for him to have a fiancée other than Carol Stanfield, and as soon as he had her out of his hair Lucy knew she would be released.

He turned and strolled towards her, coming to stand in front of her, and with a deliberate movement placed his glass down on the table beside the one she had used, then, straightening, looked hard at her.

'Three months should be long enough.'

'That long?' Carol must be very firmly entrenched for it to take that long for her to realise her affair with him was over. When he didn't answer her—Lucy had a feeling he never explained himself—she felt an overwhelming anger against him and his soured outlook on life. 'Women are mere playthings to you, aren't they?' she snapped furiously. 'Just something to be picked up, enjoyed for the moment, then tossed aside.' She received a long enigmatic look for her trouble, a look that said, 'What else are they good for?' Without him having to speak she felt herself answered, and flared up at him again. 'You needn't think if I agree to this ridiculous arrangement that I shall be one of your toys.' She wished it unsaid as soon as she had said it—there had not been the smallest hint that he had anything of that sort in mind, and she went red as she waited for his daunting comment she knew was to come. She wasn't disappointed.

'Allow me to tell you, Miss Carey,' he said loftily, 'that I'm more choosey than the Donalds of this world.'

While wanting to slap his cynical, superior face, Lucy realised she had deserved that crack. Not that she didn't think she was every bit as good as he was, she knew she was, but what else had she expected with her leading remark other than the stinging answer she had received?

With as much dignity as she could muster she rose to her feet. 'Do I have your word that if I agree to wear my mother's ring on my engagement finger for three months, at the end of that time the ring reverts to me?'

'You have my word on it.'

Bending to pick up her bag intimating that she was now ready to leave, Lucy straightened and looked directly into those cold grey-green eyes. 'In that case Mr Hemming, I accept your terms.' As yet she had no idea what pretending to be engaged to a man like him involved, but it couldn't be anything very terrible since by his own admission, and he had made it painfully clear, he was not at all interested in the romantic side of such a liaison.

He walked to the door with her, and by unspoken mutual consent the ring wasn't mentioned again—the last thing Lucy wanted was that he should go and take it from Carol and straightaway present her with it. With his hand on the door handle he paused. His face had registered very little emotion since she had entered, and it was no different now.

'For the record, my friends call me Jud. If it hurts too much, try—Judson.'

There were quite a few names she would like to have called him, and she had an idea he knew it too, but without another word being spoken, he opened the door and escorted her to the front door. She was relieved Carol Stanfield was nowhere in sight; she knew she would never have been able to look the girl in the eye.

It wasn't until the next morning that the unreality of what had taken place hit Lucy. Conscience pricked away at her as she wondered if Carol had been acquainted yet with the news that she was no longer number one in Judson Hemming's life. She must have been mad to agree to what he had suggested, Lucy thought, and she wished Rupert would get up so she could talk it over with him. It wasn't too late to go back on her word—she didn't have the ring in her possession and until she did no contract had been made. Perhaps Rupert would be able to think of some other way of getting the ring back. She had always admired the logic of his thinking—well, that was until he had taken up with Archie Proctor and his set.

Rupert hadn't returned when she had arrived home, and suspecting he would not be in any fit state to talk sensibly when he did eventually come home, Lucy had gone to bed just after midnight.

She filled in her time until she heard her brother stirring, in tidying up the sitting room. They could no longer afford domestic help and with a house this size, not to mention Rupert's untidy ways, it was a constant battle to try and keep it the way it had been kept in her mother's day when domestic help had been unlimited. She picked up a pair of Rupert's shoes from the hearth that hadn't been there when she went to bed last night while thinking that

since they had parted with quite a few items of furniture in
this room it wouldn't take long to whip round with the
vacuum cleaner.

A noise overhead told her Rupert had joined the land of
the living, and placing the shoes back in the hearth to be
taken upstairs later, she went into the kitchen to make her
brother the coffee she knew he would want more than anything when he came down.

Rupert was freshly shaven when he entered the kitchen,
only his red-rimmed eyes showing he had spent much of the
night in painting the town. Lucy thought to let him drink
his coffee first before she told him how she had spent some
of the time since she had last seen him. Without asking she
knew any offer of breakfast would be firmly rejected.

'What time is it?' he asked lazily, his head seeming too
heavy for him to lift it in the direction of the kitchen clock.

'Quarter to ten,' Lucy obliged.

'Ugh—my mouth feels like the bottom of a bird cage.
Have we any aspirin?'

Lucy fetched him the aspirin and sat down at the kitchen table with him. 'Have a nice time last night?'

'So-so. Lord, Archie Proctor can drink, took me all my
time to keep up with him.'

Knowing any discussion about Archie Proctor would end
up as had happened before, with them having cross words,
Lucy decided now was the time to tell Rupert her own
news.

'I went out myself,' she told him, and received the un-
enthusiastic brotherly response of:

'Hope your head feels better than mine this morning.'

'You know I don't drink—well, not at the rate you do,
anyway.' A few sips of champagne and one of brandy was
all the alcohol she had had yesterday, and the occasional
sherry or gin and tonic could hardly be called drinking
when matched beside the way her brother and Archie
Proctor went at it. 'Actually, I went up to Rockford Hall.'

Her brother's hand stilled as he went to reach his coffee cup for the last swallow. His head jerked round to her as though startled, and conscious that she now had his full attention, Lucy launched into details of what had happened since she had told him she had seen her ring adorning Carol Stanfield's finger.

Perhaps she should have waited until he had fully come round before she told him, Lucy thought. She suddenly noticed he was looking very pale—his poor head must be throbbing away madly, but having got so far and knowing as soon as his head cleared he would go out and she might not see him again that day, she carried on, ending with, '... so if I want to have Mother's ring back, I've got to pretend to be engaged to this Jud Hemming for three months.'

Rupert had heard her out without saying anything, and as she looked at him and waited for what he had to say on the subject, she was pleased to see some colour was returning to his cheeks—his head must be clearing.

'Well?' she prompted. He was certainly slow this morning. She hadn't quite expected him to say he would go straightaway up to the Hall and demand his sister's property back without conditions, but some sort of expression of anger against the man who was so uncaring of anyone's feelings but his own was certainly in order. 'What do you think, Rupe?' she tried again. 'Do you think we ought to go to the police anyway?'

'No.' Rupert's reply came back sharply as though her last sentence had suddenly brought him wide awake. 'No— I don't think so, Lucy,' he added more slowly. 'As you said yourself, this Jud Hemming will contest any claim we make —I mean, it isn't as if Mother wore that ring very often, and apart from Aunt Dorothy who you know as well as I hasn't seen the ring for donkey's years, there's only the two of us who can say with any conviction that it belongs in our family—and I'm none too sure I would know it alongside a similar one—besides which, when word gets out that we haven't two ha'pennies to rub together it will be thought we've latched on to this idea to get some quick money.'

'Nobody will believe that of us,' Lucy protested indignantly.

'Won't they?' Rupert shrugged cynically. 'I hate to shatter your illusions, love, but people are always ready to believe the worst—wasn't that your sole reason for going to the Hall in the first place, because you knew how gossip would stick round here if you went to the police first? In any case this Hemming chap is loaded—he owns Hemming Aluminium.' Lucy hadn't known that. Rupert must have gleaned that information last night, because he hadn't mentioned it when she'd told him about the new owner of the Hall yesterday. But she didn't have to think very hard to recall that Hemming Aluminium had factories all over the place, or need Rupert's, 'Who would believe us against him?' to know no one would.

Rupert's eyes left her face to stare into the cold remains of his coffee, and more for something to do than anything else Lucy got up and tipped the dregs away before refilling his cup, pouring coffee for herself at the same time and returning to sit at the table with him once more.

'So you think I should carry this—this thing through?' she asked after some moments' silence, feeling slightly let down that her brother hadn't come up with anything to get her off the hook.

'I don't see why you shouldn't,' Rupert said thoughtfully. 'It's only for three months after all, and after that time you'll be able to keep your ring—you said yourself it's only a mock engagement, so you've got nothing to worry about there ...' He stopped, and for the first time showed the brotherly aggression she had been looking for all along. 'He hasn't tried any—er—funny business, has he?'

It was a relief to know that Rupert wasn't so unconcerned as she had been beginning to think he was. By 'funny business' she knew he meant had Jud Hemming

made a pass at her. 'Oh no—nor is he likely to, he made
that very plain.' The way he had made it plain still stung
sufficiently for her not to want to recount to her brother
that her mock-fiancé was too choosey to want to court her
charms. 'He's too cold anyway to need the warmth of a
more than superficial involvement,' she told him.

'Then you've got nothing to worry about, have you?'
Rupert drained his second cup and looked ready to move.

Lucy realised there was no more to be said on the subject of Judson Hemming, though she would have been prepared to talk about it all day if she thought there was a way
to be found of getting her out of this entanglement. Putting
all thoughts of her mock-fiancé behind her, she judged
Rupert was now fit enough to be given his post that had
arrived that morning.

'I think there's one there from the bank,' she said tentatively, as she handed him a couple of bills and the long
white envelope.

Rupert scarcely glanced at the bills and he seemed to
know what the white envelope contained, for he folded it in
two and pushed it into his trouser pocket without reading
it. 'I'd better go along to the bank and see what old
Arbuthnot wants,' he said, getting to his feet. 'Probably
wants to tell me "This can't go on, Rupert my boy",' he
mimicked Charles Arbuthnot's tones. 'Though the account
should look better since I paid in . . .' he broke off, and Lucy
realised he had been half talking to himself.

'You've paid some money in?' She seized on the hope
that Rupert had found some cash from somewhere.

Rupert looked at her worried eyes, and his voice took on
pompous tones as he put his thumbs into an imaginary
waistcoat. 'Little girls shouldn't concern themselves with
such things,' he said grandly, and went out.

It was so good to see Rupert acting the goat again that
Lucy laughed, and it was not until his car had disappeared

out of sight that she realised he hadn't answered her question.

She fell to wondering how bad things were at the bank, wondering not for the first time if she shouldn't try and find some form of paid employment. The housework kept her busy enough, but Rupert's allowance, while sufficient for his own use, had never been intended to keep the house going, nor, she mentally added, to keep her. She had loads of clothes in her wardrobe upstairs, clothes bought when her parents had been alive when money had seemed plentiful, so she wouldn't need to buy anything new for years, but the last thing she wanted was to be a drain on her brother—yet he was adamant that she shouldn't go out to work. Rupert was full of stiffnecked pride when it came to their standing in the community, and it was pride alone she knew that was his reason for being against the idea of her finding a job. Once it became known that Rupert Carey's sister had taken a paying job it wouldn't be long before speculations began circulating about their financial position. All the same, if he came back with a glum face after seeing Mr Arbuthnot, then like it or not she was going to broach the subject again—the trouble was she wasn't trained to do anything very much.

Lucy was in the garden hanging out some washing of Rupert's she had rinsed through when Jud Hemming came to the rear of the house later that morning to find her. Her hands were damp from pegging out the washing and she wiped them down the sides of her jeans and went to meet him. She hadn't heard his car coming up the drive, but reasoned if he had come in the Bentley she wouldn't have heard its almost silent engine anyway. What he thought about the sight of the fiancée of the head of Hemming Aluminium doing the domesticated chore of putting shirts and underwear out to dry, she didn't know, but told herself she didn't care very much either—but she would far rather have been immaculately turned out in one of her smart day dresses when next she saw him. As it was, her confidence needed a definite boost as she neared him and noted that he looked different today dressed as he was in dark slacks and lightweight sweater. Her heart began to beat uncomfortably as she realised he had most likely come to hand over the ring. She should have been ready for his visit, she realised too late; it had been on the cards that she would see him again soon.

She saw him give her figure a cursory examination. If he liked what he saw—and she knew her figure to be pretty trim—it didn't show in his face.

'Good morning,' she greeted him when she was almost level with him. Her formal mode of greeting kept their association on the strictly formal basis she felt would help to get her through the next three months. He acknowledged her greeting with the merest inclination of his head. 'I'll just take this into the kitchen,' she said, indicating the wicker laundry basket she had picked up automatically and brought with her as she came down the garden path.

Still unspeaking, he followed her inside the house, and when she thought he would have waited in the hall for her to deposit the basket before conducting him into the sitting room, she turned to find he had followed her into the kitchen.

'We'll talk in the sitting room, shall we?' Dislike him she certainly did, but good manners were part and parcel of her upbringing, and while he was a guest in her home she would force herself to be polite to him.

'This room is as good as any,' he opined, and came further into the room, his very action saying he was again taking the lead.

Lucy tried to let nothing of how his arrogant attitude affected her show in her face. She liked the big old-fashioned kitchen herself, but would have preferred the more fitting surrounds of the sitting room in which to take her ring from him. The kitchen would give the whole procedure a more friendly atmosphere than she would have liked, and since there was neither warmth nor friendship between them ...

'Can I get you a coffee?' she enquired after tense seconds, when he had said nothing. Well, she couldn't ask him outright for her ring and then ask him to go, she excused herself.

'No, thanks.'

His cool refusal left her wondering what she did now. The small act of making him a drink would have given her something to do while he got round to the reason for his visit.

'Er—you haven't changed your mind about—er—what we discussed yesterday?' She could have kicked herself as soon as the words left her lips. Why did she have to hesitate, for goodness' sake? It was purely a business transaction—why couldn't she see it in that light instead of stammering like a fourteen-year-old and getting embarrassed about the whole thing.

Jud Hemming, it was obvious, felt no embarrassment whatsoever, and had no difficulty at all in calling their arrangement by its proper name. 'Our engagement, you mean?' She'd been right about his eyes, she thought as she flicked him a hasty glance and away again. They were cold, icy cold. 'No, I haven't changed *my* mind. Are you saying that you *have*—that you've thought it over and have now decided your mother's ring doesn't have the value for you that you thought it had?' Not only was there ice in his eyes, it was there in his voice too, and she had a definite conviction that no one had ever gone back on a deal with him *ever*. 'If those sort of thoughts have been flitting through your mind, you can forget them,' he confirmed her suspicion that, the bargain struck, he had no intention of allowing her to back out. 'You agreed to be engaged to me for three months—you'll go through with it right up to the very last day.'

Had he said those words in anger, she might have been able to dismiss the ominous ring to them as something said in the heat of the moment, but with each word stated so coldly, so absolutely without heat, Lucy felt fear strike within her that she was now committed, and that whatever happened during the next three months, there would be no getting out of it.

CHAPTER THREE

'WELL,' Jud Hemming demanded when Lucy felt too tense to bring herself to answer him, 'is it your intention to try and wriggle out of it?' His tone was contemptuous now as if he thought that any promise made by a member of her sex was worthless.

'As you've just stated,' Lucy replied bravely, the hostility in the room almost tangible, 'there would be very little point in my trying to "wriggle out of it". I meant what I said yesterday—I want my ring back, and if the only way that can be achieved is by temporarily wearing it as your fiancée, then I'll do it.' Her voice was almost as cold as his as she flung the words at him. 'I've never gone back on my word in my life.'

'See that you don't,' he said sharply, and putting his hand in his pocket, he withdrew the well remembered small square box and placed it on the kitchen table in front of her. 'That seals our bargain, I think,' he told her, and turned to go.

But even wanting him out of her sight as quickly as possible, Lucy wasn't avaricious, so wanting to take up the ring box, to open it, to gaze once more upon her mother's most cherished possession, she found herself asking:

'How is Carol?' and could have bitten her tongue out when Jud Hemming turned round and fixed her with a cool stare. 'I . . . I mean—was she very upset?' Her voice trailed off to a whisper as the look on his face showed her he thought her question in very poor taste.

'Why should you care? You've got what you wanted, haven't you?'

Lucy bit her lip. Yes, she'd got what she wanted, but unlike him, she was human enough to feel regret that by her doing so someone else must be terribly upset, even though in her view Carol had had a lucky escape. She tried to imagine anyone actually being married to this cold emotionless man, and only just managed to suppress a shudder at the thought.

'Yes, I've got what I wanted,' she was forced to agree, and lifted her head to tell him. 'But I can't say that being the cause of causing someone else pain fills me with any great pleasure.'

'It upsets you to think of Carol weeping her heart out?'

Poor Carol, Lucy thought, squirming inwardly at the picture that came to mind of the girl who had been so friendly to her actually breaking down in front of this man who would in all probability have been unmoved by her tears. She turned away from him so he shouldn't see the remorse in her face—he'd said it was too late to back out now, but ...

'If it's any comfort to you, Carol has known from the outset that there was never any likelihood of our ending up as marriage partners.'

'But she was still upset when you asked for the return of the ring.'

'Not at all,' he assured her, his tones none the warmer for all he was making her feel a little bit better for her part in all of this. 'It was never my intention to give the ring to her—she knew that, and only wore it because she liked it.'

While Lucy believed what he was saying—he was much too sure of himself to ever need lie about anything—she couldn't help wondering at his leaving a ring he had paid three thousand pounds for lying around for Carol to calmly pick up and place on her finger. Then again, the thought entered her mind, three thousand pounds meant nothing to him.

'Does anyone else have to know—about us, I mean?' She had been chewing this over on and off before his visit, and while he might not be the most forthcoming man in the world at least he had unbent sufficiently to tell her that Carol had known she would never be walking down the aisle with him.

'You want to keep our engagement a secret?'

Lucy winced at the word engagement. 'Well, apart from Carol, there'll be no need for anyone else to know, will there? I mean, it doesn't affect anyone else but the three of us, does it?'

Lucy liked people who looked at you when they were talking to you, but could have wished he wouldn't fix her with that hard steady stare so often. It made her feel uncomfortable, made her feel as though he was looking into the very heart of her as if he was intrigued to know what went on inside of her, what made her tick.

'No, it doesn't affect anyone but us,' he said quietly, and on that enigmatic note, without fully answering her question, he turned and left her.

He really was the strangest of men, she reflected as she waited some minutes to be sure he had gone before she picked up the ring box. A law unto himself, she considered, he did exactly what he wanted to do regardless of how other people might feel, answered only those questions he thought in need of an answer, and had now left her not knowing whether or not she had his word that he would keep their engagement a secret, or if he had plans to announce it to anyone who might be interested.

On thinking about it, Lucy decided he wouldn't tell anyone else. Why should he? All he was concerned with was getting rid of Carol—no, he wouldn't be telling anyone because in three months' time he would only have to make it known that the engagement was off. Lucy took the ring box up from the table and opened it, then took the ring from its velvet couch, handling it lovingly. A wave of emotion gripped her as she gazed at the exquisite setting of the knot of emeralds and diamonds, and Jud Hemming was forgotten as bittersweet memories of her mother took all other thoughts from her mind.

Some time during the afternoon Lucy answered the phone to hear her brother telling her he would not be home that night. To ask him where he was going and with whom would get her nowhere, she was beginning to learn, and she longed for the days before her parents had died when Rupert's life had been an open book.

'I'm going to the races with Archie,' Rupert volunteered when Lucy had shown only mild interest in his comings and goings. Her heart dipped—Archie Proctor again! 'Archie has a nag running—if it wins, and Archie is sure it's going to, we'll be celebrating afterwards, so we've booked rooms at one of the hotels just in case.'

Well, it was a weight off her mind to know Rupert wasn't going to drive home after celebrating, Lucy thought, as she put down the phone. And as the afternoon wore on she wished for the umpteenth time that Rupert had never taken up with Archie Proctor. Their father had gambled away most of Rupert's heritage; she just prayed that as well as inheriting Brook House from his father, Rupert had not inherited his gambling streak as well. She shook the thought away, but it came back to haunt her again and again as afternoon gave way to early evening, she couldn't quite see Rupert at the races, *and* with Archie Proctor, and not having a bet on one of the horses.

She set about making herself a salad with the long evening stretching before her. There were plenty of people she knew in Priors Channing, but she had no wish to call any of them, though she knew most of the evening would be spent in worrying what Rupert, with Archie Proctor as ringleader, would be up to.

In the act of giving a lettuce close scrutiny as she washed it, Lucy turned off the kitchen tap to hear the sound of a vehicle coming up the drive. Hastily she dried her hands and hurried into the hall. Rupert had decided not to stay

away overnight after all, was her first heartening thought as
she reached the front door and flung it open. But it was
not Rupert's two-seater sports car that came to a standstill
in front of the house. It was a sports car, admitted, but a
larger, more expensive model than the one Rupert owned,
and the man who was now swinging himself on to the
shingled drive was not Rupert at all, but none other than
her mock-fiancé—Jud Hemming. What he could want she
had no idea, but as she waited for him to join her at the
front door, the smile of welcome that had been for Rupert
disappeared.

'I wondered if you'd be in,' said Jud, as he came up to
her. 'I meant to mention this morning that I would prefer
it if you didn't date anybody while you're engaged to me.'

The problem of whether to accept invitations from any
of the men of her acquaintance hadn't struck her before,
and now that he mentioned it she could see it was certainly
something she would have to think about, but for him to
call at her home and calmly announce that part of their
bargain was that she declined any invitations from the
opposite sex during the next three months had small sparks
of anger spitting within her.

'That's what you've come to tell me, is it?' she asked,
her voice becoming heated. 'Well, let me tell you, Mr
Hemming . . .'

'Jud,' he broke in. 'The name's Jud, remember?' he repeated, resting his gaze on the smooth creaminess of her
skin, his eyes not missing the fire she was struggling to
hold down. 'That isn't the only reason I came to see you,'
he added coolly, and looked quietly at her, not saying another word until Lucy was forced, by his unspoken message
that he had no intention of discussing anything with her on
the doorstep, to invite him in.

She led the way into the sitting room, seeing the room as
he no doubt would view it. It was a large room, a room large
enough to take far more furniture than it housed. The

three-piece suite looked lost in it, Lucy thought, but he couldn't know having never been in the room before that it hadn't always been this sparsely furnished, she comforted herself, though he would know the few ornaments dotted about were of not much value. He couldn't know, sharp as he undoubtedly was, that the more valuable pieces of porcelain had been sold, she thought, and she knew his first glance had catalogued the room.

Jud Hemming didn't comment on the room, in fact he looked as though it didn't matter much to him in which room he said what he had come to say— it flashed through her mind he had been equally at home in the kitchen that morning. 'May I?' he asked, indicating one of the chairs.

'Yes, of course,' Lucy replied, having been so taken up with what he might be thinking about the room that she had for the moment forgotten her manners. He waited until she too was seated before taking the chair nearest to him, and she was struck to think she liked this common courtesy. She ousted the thought that she liked anything about him as it came to her that by being seated it looked as though this wasn't going to be a brief call.

'Your brother not in?' he enquired, looking relaxed as he sat back in his chair.

'No,' Lucy answered, sitting on the edge of hers. Then because that short answer had him looking at her questioningly, 'He won't be back tonight. Did you want to see him?'

'Does he often stay away overnight?'

It wasn't anything to do with him what Rupert did, and that was another question he hadn't deigned to answer, not that she could think of any good reason why he should want to see her brother.

'He's twenty-five, he can make his own decision whether he comes home or not.' She felt aggression rising on her brother's behalf.

'And how old are you, Lucy?' he asked smoothly, ignoring her aggression.

'Twenty-two.' She hadn't wanted to answer but couldn't see any good reason why he shouldn't know how old she was. 'How old are you?' She didn't see why he should be the one to ask all the questions.

'Thirty-five,' he supplied. 'You don't mind that your brother goes off and leaves you here on your own—you're quite isolated here and you don't have any live-in staff, do you?'

'We don't have any staff at all,' she said shortly before it came to her that he knew anyway, and that his reference to 'live-in staff' had been his tactful way of saying she was there completely on her own. She had never associated him with such sensitivity, and it had her rising out of her chair and asking him merely for something to say to get off the subject, 'Would you care for a drink?'

She subsided into her chair again as with, 'No, thanks,' he refused, then looking at her steadily, he said quietly, 'Since you appear to be all on your own this evening, perhaps you would like to come back with me and have dinner?'

'Up at the Hall?' The question was out when she had no intention of going any further than the front door with him.

'At the Hall,' he confirmed.

'No, thanks.' It was a pleasure to turn down his invitation even though she had no idea what had motivated his issuing it—it wasn't from any desire to have her company, of that she was positive. Was it, she wondered, his way of ensuring she didn't date anybody else while she was engaged to him? If he thought ...

'That's a pity,' he broke in on her thoughts. 'My mother was looking forward to your joining us for dinner.'

'Your mother?' Lucy gasped, her surprise showing as her dark brown eyes opened wide. 'Does ... Your mother doesn't know about—us, does she?'

'She does.'

His confirmation in those two controlled words had her rising out of her chair, only to find he had risen too. 'How could you tell her?' she demanded angrily. 'I thought we agreed not to say anything to anybody.' They hadn't agreed exactly, she remembered after the words had left her lips. In fact she remembered clearly that Jud had left before she'd been able to get any sort of answer from him.

'I don't recall agreeing to keep our engagement secret,' he said shortly. 'But for your information, it wasn't I who told my mother—I think I can say I was as surprised as she when she came home after having had tea with Mrs Arbuthnot and said how pleased everyone was that Lucy Carey was marrying her son. I think my mother would have appreciated hearing the news first hand from me rather than have the bank manager's wife pass on the information.'

His voice sounded hard and inflexible, and Lucy groaned inwardly. She remembered the older woman who had stood with him, Carol and Joyce Appleby yesterday; she had been totally unlike her son in looks, Lucy recalled, having a more gentle look to her. She thought she knew exactly what must have happened, and wished she had thought to tell Rupert not to mention her engagement to anyone. But she hadn't thought it necessary, hadn't thought at all if it came to that, believing that Rupert, knowing the circumstances of her engagement, would want to keep it as quiet as she herself. It had never dawned on her that he would go and tell Mr Arbuthnot that his sister was engaged to the owner of Rockford Hall. Poor Mrs Hemming, she must have been dreadfully hurt at receiving the news from a stranger.

Lucy looked up and across to where Jud Hemming was standing. His look was chilling and she hoped she never knew him when he let go of his temper. That would be a truly formidable sight—and experience—for the person on the receiving end; she only hoped he would hold on to his temper long enough for her to apologise.

'I ... I'm very sorry, Mr—Jud,' she managed at last. 'I'm very sorry your mother heard about—us this way. I'm afraid I must take the blame.' She looked away from him as his eyes iced over. 'I told Rupert everything this morning, and he went to see Mr Arbuthnot later—I can only suppose my brother told the bank manager and he relayed it to his wife——' Her voice faded and she ended lamely, 'I never thought to tell Rupert not to say anything to anyone.'

Silence greeted her confession, and still unable to look at Jud, Lucy stared at the crisp white shirt he had on beneath his dark jacket. Then the shirt was coming nearer to her, and she lifted startled brown eyes to his face as two strong hands were raised and came to rest on her shoulders.

'It would appear that since everyone in Priors Channing will soon know of our engagement, the bargain is well and truly sealed.' His eyes were glinting down at her, and Lucy felt fear streak through her as he hauled her up against him until their bodies were touching. 'I think under the circumstances I can be forgiven if I take some of the dubious pleasures of that bargain,' he told her, his voice none the warmer for what she was terrified he was about to do. Her own voice felt bolted up inside of her, making her powerless to say anything to dissuade him from his intent. Then before she could begin to struggle away from him, his head came down, the mouth she had thought so hard was against her own, and as their lips met the hardness left his mouth and became a warm, searching mouth that surprised her as much as the situation she now found herself in.

Pushing against his chest was useless, she found. Jud Hemming was kissing her as if he meant it, and there was no way he was going to let her go until he had assuaged the cold anger in him. The worst thing about it was, Lucy thought as she struggled, that the mastery of his kisses was having the oddest effect on her. If she didn't dislike him so very much, she would, she thought, have found the experience quite enjoyable.

This thought alone had sufficient strength for her to give one gigantic push, which happened to coincide with what must, she thought, be Jud's own opinion that he had had enough, for she found herself free of him with the space of a yard or so separating them.

A mixture of emotions rioted through her as she found herself free of him. His face was looking as unconcerned as ever, but to her regret, the best she could come out with as she whipped anger into every word was a sarcastic:

'I thought you said you were choosey.'

'Stung, did it?' he enquired coolly, in no way put out by her anger. Lucy looked away from him. If she could be sure he wouldn't try that trick again she would have turned her back on him, but she wasn't taking any chances. 'You have no need to worry,' his voice reached her, 'I'm not likely to kiss you again.' His tone indicated that he thought once was enough for any man, which had her wanting to fly at him. Only with the greatest of effort did she restrain herself. Then out of the blue he asked, 'Where's your engagement ring?'

It irritated her that he should refer to it as her 'engagement ring'. 'In my bag,' she replied shortly, and found herself commanded:

'Put it on.'

Lucy could see little point in arguing. As he had said, the bargain was well and truly sealed, and in any case she had a feeling if she didn't voluntarily 'put it on', Jud Hemming would slip the ring over her knuckle if it meant he had to break her finger to do so. Going over to the side of the settee, she picked up her bag and delved into it to extract the ring. As she knew it would, it fitted.

'Anything else?' she asked, and wanted to add 'sir' but thought better than to risk it, for all she was no longer afraid of him.

'Yes,' he answered. 'Make sure you're wearing it when I introduce you to my mother.'

'Intro ... You don't think I'm coming back with you, do you—not after that ...'

'Good God, you'll be telling me next you've never been kissed before,' he interrupted her scoffingly.

'I've been kissed many times before,' Lucy returned smartly, 'and always enjoyed it *before*.'

She expected some stinging sarcasm to come hurtling her way for that '*before*', but to her utter amazement she saw she had amused him, saw for the first time a hint of amusement in his face, quickly gone, as he said, 'You may have been kissed many times, but you still have a lot to learn,' then went on in a different tone, 'I think it only fair, Lucy, in view of the hurt my mother received today, that you come with me and meet her.'

He couldn't have said anything more calculated to get her to agree to go with him. She could fully understand, Lucy thought, the pain his mother must have felt at having someone outside the family telling her of her son's engagement.

'Have you told your mother our engagement will end in three months' time?' she questioned.

'I think she's had enough hurt for one day,' Jud told her. 'She's old-fashioned enough to believe in love, and is tickled pink at the idea that I've at last found the "right one".' Not without much searching and sampling either, I'll bet, Lucy wanted to put in, but thought better of it, though Jud's lips twitched again briefly, which gave her an idea he knew exactly what she was thinking. 'I would rather she kept her illusions for the time being,' he went on, no sign of humour on his face now. 'She hasn't been well— seeing me ensnared seems to have put new life into her.' He paused, then with his eyes not leaving her face, asked bluntly, 'Well, will you come?'

'Have I any choice?' She didn't expect an answer, which

was just as well, because she didn't get one.

Up in her bedroom Lucy would have loved to dawdle as she dressed herself ready to meet Jud's mother. She was being contrary, she knew, but it still irked her at having to give in to his order that she have dinner up at the Hall— as she had already told him, she reflected as she shook out a pale apricot-coloured dinner gown prior to stepping into it, she had had very little choice. No choice either when Jud Hemming had elected to wait downstairs while she changed. Oh, she'd tried to get rid of him, but her, 'I'll be ready if you call back for me in an hour,' had had him replying, 'You'll be ready in half that time, and I'll wait right here.' His eyes had been cold as he had surveyed her then, and she had slammed up to the bathroom to take a quick shower with the very definite feeling that if she was one minute over the half hour, she would hear his footsteps charging up the stairs to get her. Oh damn, now her zip had stuck.

Backing towards the mirror, Lucy struggled to see where the metal had caught the fine apricot material. The minutes ticked on as she wrestled with the recalcitrant zip, but all she achieved was to jam it so tight it would go neither up nor down. Marvellous, she thought, sitting down on her dressing table stool and staring glum-faced at her reflection; she would have to ask that brute downstairs to take a look at it because the zip had stuck so fast she couldn't even take the dress off and put on something else. Fortunately her face was made up and her hair smoothly brushed and swinging loosely to her shoulders; she was ready apart from that stupid zip. She listened thinking she heard a movement downstairs and considered that was all she needed for Jud Hemming to start to become impatient. Standing up, she slewed round and saw in the mirror the expanse of bare back that would be open to his view if she asked him to see if he could fix her zip.

With the resigned thought of 'what else can I do?' she

left her bedroom and as she reached the head of the stairs
saw that Jud had come out into the hall and was looking up
at her from the bottom of the stairs. Even from that dis-
tance the expression on his face looked distinctly chilly.

'Ready?' he called, when she made no move to join him.

'No,' she called back, and before she could add anything
further, the intimacy of the request she had to make causing
her to hesitate to voice it, Jud did no more than begin to
ascend the stairs. 'You can't come up here,' she protested,
wasting her breath as he joined her on the landing.

'Your half hour is up,' he told her icily. 'You look ready
and you've already agreed to come—so don't start playing
games with me at this stage. I warn you now ...'

'My zip's stuck,' Lucy cut in, not liking the ominous
threat behind his words.

Jud looked at the front of her, seemed to notice only then
that the front of her bodice was not fitting as snugly as it
might have done, and that her dress had never been de-
signed to reveal any part of her breasts, the creamy swell
now open to his gaze. 'Turn around,' he instructed coolly,
clearly unaffected by the sight of her charms, and unspeaking Lucy did as she was bidden. 'The light's no good here,'
he said after a moment or two. 'Let's try your bedroom.'

'The light is better downstairs,' Lucy lied, feeling un-
accountably nervous at having this suddenly still man in
the intimate closeness of her bedroom.

'Believe it or not,' said Jud, as the silence lengthened
between them, 'I'm more interested in having my dinner
at this moment than taking advantage of anything you have
to offer.'

Stung once more by his sarcasm, his very tone telling
her whatever else other men might think of her, she left
him cold, Lucy stormed ahead of him, mindless that he had
a clear view of her, as her flapping dress fell off her shoulders to reveal a goodly proportion of her naked back. She
left him to please himself whether he followed her into her

room, and stood silently fuming with her dress held to the front of her her back to the open door. She didn't care then whether her dress was mended or not; one more word out of him and he could return to the Hall by himself.

Lucy knew the instant he came into the room and her body tensed when she felt his hands warm on her back. 'Relax,' the quietly spoken word reached her. 'I can't do a thing while you're trembling so badly.' Up to that point she hadn't been aware she had been trembling; it was pure fury of course that had got her into this state. 'I've said I won't take advantage—surely that bit of a kiss downstairs hasn't unnerved you to this extent?'

Bit of a kiss? She wouldn't want to know him when he really got going! 'I've had better than that from novices,' she told him coldly, and only as the words dropped from her lips and all movement behind her ceased did she realise her words had sounded challenging. The last thing she wanted, she hurriedly realised, was that Jud Hemming should give her a further demonstration that he had passed out of the Lovemaking Academy with first class honours. 'I didn't mean that,' she retracted quickly, terrified suddenly at the lack of movement behind her. 'Y . . . you've got me so confused I don't know what I'm saying.'

'Confused?' She heard his voice at last, quietly dropping the question into the tension-filled air.

'I . . . I . . . Oh, put it down to the fact that I'm not used to having a man in my bedroom,' she said irritably, and wished he would hurry up and fix her zip so they could get out of her room and the intimacy that surrounded them.

She felt Jud's hands come to rest on her shoulders, causing her head to jerk upright as his grip tightened. 'You're no stranger to bedroom scenes, though, are you?' he asked, his voice sounding offhand in her ears, as though he wasn't really interested in her reply.

'As you stated previously,' she told him, 'I still have a lot to learn.'

The sudden increased pressure on her shoulders worried her, but it lasted no longer than two seconds, then Jud's hands left her shoulders and he was once more trying to free her zip, saying coolly, 'In that case I'd better hurry up and get this job done so that we can leave your chaste little room,' and then infuriatingly, when he must know any movement she made would have her dress tearing at the seams, he added, 'If you have me in mind to be your tutor, forget it—cut your teeth on somebody else.'

It could have been his way of assuring her she had nothing to fear from him, but Lucy didn't see it like that; she knew he had taken her 'I still have a lot to learn' as an invitation, an invitation he had turned down, and her fury threatened to boil over. Then her zip was sliding up, Jud having achieved the job he set out to do, and she was left staring at the door as he went out saying, 'I'll wait for you downstairs.'

He was absolutely, one hundred per cent *insufferable*! Lucy thought as she collected her wrap. It was a warm night, and her wrap wouldn't be needed, but she felt in need of holding something in her hands; she didn't trust her control sufficiently to have her hands free if Jud Hemming made another crack like the last one before they reached the Hall.

Mrs Hemming came out into the hall to greet them when she heard them arrive and within a very few minutes Lucy decided she liked Jud's mother very much. How could she not like her when she was so opposite from her son, not only in looks but in manner too?

'I thought you were never going to get here,' she said after Jud had introduced them. 'Forgive my impatience, Lucy, but I've so looked forward to this day.'

Lucy summoned up a smile as she walked with the grey-haired woman, who was about her own height, into the drawing room she had been in only yesterday. She found it difficult to meet Mrs Hemming's eyes while they sipped sherry before going in to dinner, and this upset her because she had never had any trouble looking directly at anyone before. It was guilt, pure and simple, she knew, at the deception she and Jud were practising on this welcoming woman, that kept her looking down into her lap for most of the time. She hoped Mrs Hemming would put it down to shyness until she could get a grip on herself.

During dinner conversation became more general, and Lucy was thankful to be able to appear more natural. This was Mrs Hemming's first visit to Rockford Hall since her son had moved in, and she was interested in everything Lucy could tell her about the district and its inhabitants.

'It's lovely hearing everything from someone who's lived in the neighbourhood for a long time,' Mrs Hemming said at one stage. 'Jud can't abide the sort of affair we went to yesterday morning. He'd bought tickets, of course, to support the charity, but I made him take me so that I could get to know as many people as I could while I'm here.'

The conversation moved on to something else and Lucy drew a relieved breath that with the strawberries and champagne function successfully out of the way, she hadn't had to reveal she had been there too. She was grateful now that there had been such a crush and she had not got around to meeting Jud's mother then—she would like to have seen Jud lie his way out of that one. Then what Mrs Hemming had just said about wanting to get to know as many people as she could while she was here made her ask:

'You don't live at the Hall?'

'Oh no, didn't Jud tell you?' Lucy looked down at her plate as she tried to find a suitable answer that didn't involve the need to lie to this kindly woman. Then there was no need to lie, for Mrs Hemming was saying, 'Of course he hasn't, I expect you've been too wrapped up in each other to think of anything else,' and went on to tell her she had a house in Malvern. Originally she and Jud had lived in Warwickshire, and although they had liked the area very

much, there was nothing to compare with the pre-
Cambrian hills of Malvern. She had visited them often as
a girl, and when Jud's hard work had paid off and he told
her he would buy her a house anywhere in the world she
chose to live, there had been no other choice for her but
Malvern. 'Not many mothers are blessed with such wonderful sons,' Mrs Hemming said, giving Jud an affection-
ate smile.

'You're biased,' Jud told his mother.

'So I expect is Lucy,' his mother replied proudly.

'Not every girl of my acquaintance falls in love with me,
you know,' Jud said indulgently.

'Ah, but Lucy did—didn't you, my dear?'

Conscious that two pairs of eyes were turned in her
direction, Lucy felt the heat of a blush creep up under her
skin.

'Now you've made her blush,' Jud put in quietly, and
deftly changed the subject to talk about the redecorations
he had planned for some of the upstairs rooms.

After a delicious meal where the main course had been
one of Lucy's favourites, duck superbly cooked with an
orange sauce, they adjourned to the drawing room where
a trim little maid came in with a tray of coffee.

Inevitably it seemed, with Mrs Hemming so pleased
about her son's engagement, talk came round once more to
this subject. Mrs Hemming handed Lucy a cup of coffee,
remarking, 'Have you named the day yet, Lucy?'

Lucy took tight hold of her coffee cup and saucer, staring at the steaming liquid as though fascinated, only lifting her eyes when Jud told his mother softly:

'Lucy's parents died quite recently—we've decided to
wait awhile.'

'Oh, my dear, I am sorry!' Mrs Hemming's sympathy
was instant, and knowing that since she was deceiving her
so badly she didn't deserve her sympathy, Lucy had to
blink hard to keep the tears away. She didn't like that Jud

should use her dead parents as a means to get her out of a
tension-filled moment, but she realised with a fairness she
didn't want to feel that there was very little else he could
have said that would sound convincing. 'Are you all alone
now?' Mrs Hemming enquired gently, and Lucy with her
control returning was able to tell her she lived with her
brother Rupert, and had an aunt living in Garbury, a pretty
little village on the outskirts of Sheffield.

Towards ten o'clock Jud decided it was time his mother
was tucked up in bed. 'Dr Reading said you must keep
regular hours and I think you've had enough excitement
for one day,' he told her.

'You're marrying a bully,' Mrs Hemming smiled across
at the dark-haired girl she thought would one day be her
daughter-in-law. 'I shall see you again before I go back,
shan't I?' she asked.

Jud handed his mother her handbag, making some comment to the effect that he was sure it had a hundredweight
of coal in it, it was so heavy, and was it necessary for her to
carry so much about with her, to which Mrs Hemming replied that men didn't understand about such matters, and
gratefully Lucy realised there was no need for her to answer
the question Mrs Hemming had put to her, while wishing
the circumstances of their meeting had been different because Jud's mother was proving to be as good and kind as
her own mother had been.

'Jud's taking me back to Malvern on Friday,' Mrs Hemming told her. 'There isn't very much time for us to get to
know each other very well.' She thought for a brief pause,
then turned to her son and suggested warmly, 'Jud, why
don't you and Lucy come and stay with me for the weekend? You could do with a break, I'm sure, and a weekend
in the Malverns will blow all the cobwebs away.'

Her words dropped into a tense silence on Lucy's part
as she waited for Jud to answer for them both. She didn't
know how he was going to get them out of going, but he

would she was sure. He would see, she was certain, that to
deceive his mother for the few hours she had been in her
company at the Hall had been difficult enough. To spend
the weekend with her at her home would be too much—
apart from the distaste she felt at the deception, she would
never be able to play her part convincingly for a whole
weekend. She felt herself relax as Jud helped his mother to
her feet and began to speak, then all her nerve ends seemed
to tighten into one outsized knot, as she heard him saying
easily:

'What an excellent idea. We'd like that very much,
wouldn't we, Lucy?'

CHAPTER FOUR

LUCY'S control was at breaking point when Jud returned after seeing his mother from the room. She was so angry she didn't trust herself to speak without yelling at him and thereby risking waking the whole house. She stood up, her lips tightly together, her handbag over her arm.

'You want to go?'

Several short sharp sentences of affirmation sprang to her lips, but she managed to bite them down. 'Yes,' she said instead, and refused to say anything else.

Jud stood looking at her; he couldn't help but notice her tight-lipped expression. He was astute enough to know she was quietly simmering, she felt sure, but if he anticipated a slanging match, he said nothing other than, 'I'll get your wrap.'

Once they were in the car and driving away from the Hall, Lucy could contain herself no longer. 'How dare you!' she ground out, her words coming out in tightly controlled fury. 'How dare you!'

'How dare I what?' Jud replied, seeming to be greatly surprised that she had taken exception to anything that had gone on that evening. 'I must confess myself mystified, Lucy, at what you've found to be angry about.'

So her seething fury had not been lost on him. 'How could you accept your mother's invitation for both of us?' she stormed, then really getting into her stride, 'You can have no idea how I felt at having to deceive her—I felt sick every time I had to lie to her . . .'

'But you didn't have to lie to her, did you?' Jud cut in, his tone still sounding unconcerned. Lucy thought for a

61

moment—he was right, she hadn't in actual fact told any lies that evening, but——

'I lied to her by implication—I've joined forces with you in allowing her to believe we're engaged.' She was silent for a brief moment, then, 'Doesn't it bother you that you've lied to her?'

'Not if the end justifies the means,' Jud said smoothly.

Lucy sat quietly fuming. What sort of man was he—this man who could calmly pretend to be engaged to her to get himself out of Carol's clutches, and carry it through even if it meant lying to his own mother?

'You should be ashamed of yourself,' she said, her thoughts on his mother, and was quite unprepared for the burst of laughter that echoed in her ears as the man by her side gave way to outrageous amusement. She could see nothing at all funny in what she had said, and although at any other time she might have thought his laughter a pleasant sound—up until then she hadn't thought he'd got a laugh in him—at that moment, the sound of his laughter made her more infuriated than ever. 'You're disgusting!' she fumed, and would have said more, only he stopped her with one well-chosen sentence.

'And you, Lucy, have the makings of a first-class shrew.'

If he hadn't been negotiating the car round a particularly tight bend she knew well, Lucy felt she would have been unable to resist the impulse to punch his head for that remark, but since he was the last person she wanted to end up in a ditch with, she used all her will power and kept her hands clenched tightly in her lap, and said not another word until he drew up outside Brook House, when he showed every sign of going in with her.

'I'll be all right on my own,' she said shortly. It was another waste of breath, she saw, as he left the car and walked to the front door with her. The house was in darkness and she fumbled in her bag for her key, only to have it taken out of her hand and inserted in the lock by Jud. It was Jud too who snicked on the light and stood to one side in the hall as she preceded him into the sitting room.

She'd be damned if she would thank him for her dinner. 'I won't be going with you to Malvern for the weekend,' she said, making no bones about it. It was a fact, she wasn't going, and he might just as well know now as later; he should never have accepted for her in the first place.

'Did you think all you had to do to earn your ring was to wear it?' he demanded.

It did seem an easy way to earn three thousand pounds' worth of sentiment, Lucy admitted then, and wondered if she would have agreed to wear it had she known the further deception she would be called upon to practice. As she looked down at her left hand the ring sparkled back at her, bringing a lump to her throat—the ring truly belonged to her, but she felt defeated suddenly.

'Don't make me go, Jud,' she said softly, all temper gone from her now, her voice unconsciously pleading.

'What's your objection to going?' Jud's voice was hard, ignoring the pleading note in her voice.

'I . . . I . . .' then as his unyielding attitude got through to her, her own voice lost some of its softness. 'I could never have deceived my own mother. You mother reminds me of her—not in the way she looks, but she has the same gentle manner, the same kind way with her . . .' her voice tapered off. What she told him was the truth, but she couldn't look at him, doubting her words would have any effect on him—he was much too hard.

She was proved right, for his voice was harder than ever when he spoke, causing her to wonder if he thought she was putting on an act just to get out of going.

'We'll be leaving on Friday afternoon,' he said coldly. 'Make sure you're ready.'

How had she got into all this? Lucy wondered as she lay wide awake in her bed after Jud had gone. It had seemed so simple at the start; all she had had to do, she had thought, was to wear the ring on her engagement finger for three months. She should have realised without having to be reminded that Jud Hemming had paid three thousand pounds for the ring, she must have been an idiot to think he would write off the loss of his money so easily. And yet if Rupert hadn't blabbed about her engagement to Charles Arbuthnot, none of this would have happened.

Thinking of her brother she hoped he was safely tucked up in bed somewhere and not getting up to any mischief with Archie Proctor. She wished she could stop this over-protective feeling she had for her brother—as she had told Jud earlier that evening, Rupert was twenty-five and well able to make his own decisions, but that didn't stop her worrying about him. He had been shaken to the core when he had discovered the lands he had hoped one day would be his had been gambled away from him, and she could understand in part why he should feel 'to hell with everything' and go wild for a time, especially since he had worked so hard to learn everything there was to know about looking after his inheritance. Poor Rupert, there was no longer an estate for him to manage.

Her thoughts see-sawed backwards and forwards between Jud Hemming and her brother, and she fell asleep at last wondering what on earth had possessed Rupert to tell the bank manager she was engaged to Jud.

Lucy felt much better about everything when she got up the next morning. Everything had seemed to have taken on nightmare proportions last night. She still didn't want to spend the weekend at Mrs Hemming's house, and had to keep taking a look at her ring every now and then to prevent herself from taking out her writing case and penning a regretful note to her saying she couldn't go. But as Jud had reminded her last night, the only lies she had told had been by implication only—that still didn't make them any less lies, in her view, but there was small consolation in that, and she did so want to keep her ring. Its monetary value

was incidental, she loved it because it had belonged to her
mother and would have loved it equally had it been worth
only a few pounds.

She was still preoccupied with her thoughts after lunch
when Rupert returned. There was no doubting he was in
high spirits as he came whistling into the kitchen where
Lucy was putting a sponge cake in the oven.

'Made a killing at the races yesterday,' he said excitedly
after the briefest of greetings. 'Old Archie put me on to a
couple of good nags ...' He then went on to explain the
intricacies of doubling one's bet by letting all the money
won on the first horse ride on the second, and then on to
more involved procedure that seemed highly complicated
to Lucy. With a sinking heart she listened to him enthuse
about 'good old Archie', and wanted to beg him to have
nothing more to do with him. She had a question she
wanted to ask her brother and it had nothing at all to do
with horses, but she held back until eventually Rupert came
to the end of his tale; he still had the light of success in his
eyes and she didn't want to take that look away—he'd had
very little to get excited about lately—but her question
couldn't wait any longer, and with the openness of the relationship she had had with him since childhood, she asked
her question straight out:

'Why did you think it necessary to tell Charles Arbuthnot that I was engaged to Jud Hemming, Rupe?'

Expecting him to at least have the grace to look ashamed
of himself, Lucy was shaken to see Rupert greet her question with no sign of looking abashed, though he did think
to say he hadn't thought old man Arbuthnot would spread
it around.

'I hadn't meant to tell him,' he admitted, not at all put
out that his sister should take him to task about it. 'But he
was treating me like a school-kid—you know the sort of
thing I mean.' Lucy said nothing and waited to hear him
out as he mimicked Charles Arbuthnot's tones and man-

nerisms. 'He reminded me, as if I needed any reminding, that "your family have always been well respected, Rupert. I know you have had to take a nasty blow, but unless you do something about clearing your overdraft I shall be forced to take steps to ensure that the bank has its money".' Lucy didn't know how Mr Arbuthnot proposed the overdraft be cleared, and privately she thought he was being a little high-handed about an amount which at the most couldn't be more than a couple of hundred pounds, but she bit her lip worriedly as Rupert went on. 'Old Arbuthnot carried on in the same vein for what seemed an hour—though I was only with him for twenty minutes—but when he said, "The last thing I want, Rupert, is that you should lose your status in the community"—well, it niggled me. Who does he think he is, for God's sake? So I told him, "Actually, Mr Arbuthnot, I think there's very little likelihood of that," and you should have seen his face, Lucy, when I told him you were engaged to the millionaire owner of Rockford Hall.'

Lucy turned away from him trying to drown her thoughts as she filled the kettle to make a cup of tea. So it had been bravado—sheer bravado, that had been the reason for Rupert telling Charles Arbuthnot she was engaged, and to whom. She wondered who else the bank manager had told besides his wife, and realised it didn't really matter who else he had told—as Jud had said, it wouldn't be long before it was all over Priors Channing anyway. Mrs Arbuthnot was not likely to keep that snippet of news to herself.

'I say, you're not upset about it, are you?' Rupert, Lucy thought, was being particularly insensitive about the whole affair.

'I was upset, Rupert,' she confessed, by calling him by his full name showing she wasn't feeling all that friendly to him just then. 'Jud Hemming came here yesterday—Mrs Arbuthnot had told Jud's mother, and he insisted I go to the Hall and be introduced to her.'

'Strewth!' muttered Rupert, taken out of his stride momentarily, only to come bouncing back to say, 'Well, you're still alive to tell the tale.'

Lucy saw it was pointless telling Rupert any of her feelings, the uncaring mood he was now in. 'Yes, I am, aren't I,' she said quietly. 'Do you want a cup of tea?'

'Might take some of the fur off my tongue,' Rupert replied, letting her know he had drunk his fill last night. She joined him at the kitchen table, and sat absentmindedly stirring her tea—she didn't take sugar.

'You'll have to look after yourself this weekend,' she stated unemotionally. 'I'm going to stay with Jud's mother for a few days on Friday.'

Rupert went up to his room shortly after he had drunk his tea. No doubt to catch up on the sleep he had missed, Lucy thought, as she rinsed the teacups they had used. Far from showing regret that she had been manoeuvred into going to Malvern on Friday, he had seemed delighted—not that she had told him how Jud had accepted the invitation for her when she had been certain he would have refused; Rupert's face, she recalled, had beamed at the news and all he had said was, 'I thought you said Jud Hemming didn't fancy you.' She hadn't used those actual words, though she had implied them, she recalled as she took the sponge cake out of the oven. Then feeling her emotions beginning to get on top of her, she tipped the cake out on to a rack to cool and went outside into the sunshine and taking a route across fields that were as familiar to her as breathing, she took herself off for a long walk, not returning until she had walked her agitated feelings out of her system.

Lucy saw nothing of Jud Hemming for the next few days, and was relieved about that. She had no idea where he worked, but since the nearest Hemming Aluminium plant was about forty miles away she reasoned that he probably went there daily. Assuming he would be working during the day, that still left him with his evenings free, but when it came to Thursday and he hadn't contacted her, she began to feel a little irritated. He was playing the lord of the manor with a vengeance, she thought. Having said he would call for her on Friday afternoon he had left it at that, as if having given his instructions he need not concern himself with her until Friday.

News of her engagement had spread rapidly round the village and she had several phone calls from friends who rang to wax enthusiastically about her good fortune. Philippa Browne was one of her telephone callers, saying she couldn't believe it when she had heard.

'I never had any inkling that a romance was going on right under my nose,' said Pippa, who always reckoned to know everything that was happening. 'Mrs Hemming was at the hairdressers at the same time I was having my hair done—I've had it done in that new frizzy style, though I don't think I like it—anyway, Mrs Hemming was saying you met her son when he first came to view the Hall, and that things grew from there. You are lucky, Lucy—I'd give my eye teeth for him, with or without his bank balance!'

Lucy had sat stunned for a while after the call. It took all sorts, she mused, thinking over what Pippa had said about giving her eye teeth for Jud Hemming. She had to admit, if she was to be truly honest, that some women might go for his cool manner—she refused to dwell on the nebulous thought that had come to her when he had kissed her, that if she didn't dislike him so much she might have enjoyed the experience; the kisses she had received prior to the ones he had bestowed had lacked the experience of the more mature man. Hastily she turned her mind away to reflect that he must have told his mother that bit about their first meeting when he had come to view the Hall. Were there no lies he wouldn't utter in order to get his own way?

On Thursday evening she had done nothing about packing her weekend case. It was as though by not doing so she felt herself uncommitted. Rupert was out again tonight, probably again with Archie Proctor. He would have told her who he was meeting if she had asked him, only like an ostrich burying its head in the sand, she had decided she didn't want to know, and in consequence now wished she had.

When the phone rang she went to answer it, wondering if it was Rupert to say he wouldn't be coming home that night. But it wasn't Rupert's voice she heard but that of Jud calling her from Germany.

'I didn't tell you what time to be ready,' he said infuriatingly.

'I've been sitting here waiting for my orders,' she came back sarcastically.

There was a small pause, and when he spoke next she thought she could detect a faint trace of amusement in his voice, but it must have been a distortion in the telephone cables, she thought, because it soon disappeared.

'You haven't been up to the Hall,' he stated.

She had no idea how long he had been in Germany, but no doubt he would have been in touch with the Hall by telephone and his mother would have told him she hadn't seen her.

'No—I'm not as practised as you in the art of lying without verbally committing myself.'

'You are committed, though, aren't you?' he jibed.

'Roll on the end of August,' Lucy retorted fervently. It was indelibly imprinted on her mind that the end of August would see the end of their engagement. 'What time shall I be ready tomorrow?' she asked into the silence left when Jud made no reply to her fervent wish.

'I'll call for you around three,' he said smoothly, then the line went dead.

Lucy was ready when the Bentley pulled up outside Brook House the following afternoon. She had been pacing up and down the sitting room carpet still trying to think up ways of getting out of going, when she spotted the car from the window. There was no one in the passenger seat, so she guessed they would be returning to the Hall to pick up Mrs Hemming.

Dressed in a linen suit of ice blue, she went to let Jud in. Rupert had gone out before lunch, and she had hoped he would be back before Jud arrived if only because it would have meant he had sufficient brotherly concern to see for himself the man she was engaged to. But Rupert hadn't returned and if she didn't know better she would have suspected he was purposely keeping out of Jud's way, which was ridiculous because the two had never met and there was no reason for Rupert to avoid meeting him.

'Ready?' asked Jud, as she opened the door to him putting his hand out for the weekend case she was holding.

Unspeaking, Lucy handed her case over, pulling the door closed behind her. It annoyed her that Jud checked to see that the door was securely locked, but she stamped down her feeling of annoyance, knowing that in ten minutes or so she would have to greet Mrs Hemming as though she hadn't a care in the world.

Jud seemed quite unconcerned that she hadn't spoken one word to him, and that irritated her further. They were almost on the point of turning into the drive of the Hall before it came to her that she might be being a little childish. She looked down at the ring on her finger. She was being well paid after all, she thought, it wouldn't hurt to be civil to him—beast that he was.

'D ... did you have a pleasant time in Germany?' she enquired politely as the car turned into the drive of the Hall, and could have wished she had been able to make her remark without that stammering start.

'You've spoilt a record,' Jud answered mysteriously.

'Record?'

'I've never known a woman be quiet for ...' he checked his watch as he halted the car outside the front door of the

Hall, '... all of ten minutes,' he ended.

'I'll bet,' said Lucy acidly, a mental picture of him with some willing female in his arms flashing unheralded through her mind. It was disconcerting to realise that Jud knew a fair bit of the thoughts that went through her mind, disconcerting also to hear that laugh she had heard once before.

She was outside the car before he had come round to her side, and was a little ashamed of herself for the way she slammed the door behind her. The majestic Bentley had done nothing to deserve such treatment.

Mrs Hemming greeted her warmly and when the time came to get into the car again Lucy went to the rear passenger door intending Mrs Hemming should sit with her son, but Mrs Hemming wouldn't hear of her occupying the rear seat.

'You sit up front with Jud,' she smiled. 'I might want to nod off.'

Suspecting that since her illness Mrs Hemming had most likely taken to having a rest every afternoon, Lucy smiled back. 'Are you sure?' she enquired, noticing now they were outside in broad daylight that Jud's mother did look a little tired.

'Quite sure, Lucy—if my eyelids do begin to droop you and Jud can carry on a conversation without worrying about disturbing me.'

Lucy got into the front seat knowing if Mrs Hemming did fall asleep, it was going to be very quiet inside the car indeed, for nothing would induce her to voluntarily say anything to Jud.

It was a glorious afternoon and once on their way Jud drove expertly and without fuss. For the first hour talk flowed easily and without restraint between Lucy and Mrs Hemming, Jud saying very little, and at one stage half turned in her seat so Mrs Hemming shouldn't have to talk to the back of her head, Lucy caught a look on his face that told her he was silently reiterating what he had said about never having known a woman keep quiet for ten minutes. Lucy found she was able to ignore him without Mrs Hemming being aware of it. Then talk between them became spasmodic and thinking perhaps Mrs Hemming might now want to sleep, Lucy turned round to face the front.

She saw the hills of Malvern long before they reached them, and as they came nearer and nearer she wondered, not for the first time, what the weekend would hold. So far everything had gone along swimmingly, and although neither she nor Jud were demonstrative with each other— God forbid—Mrs Hemming had not noticed that everything was not as it should be between two people who she thought were head over heels in love with each other. Lucy guessed that Jud wasn't the demonstrative type anyway, and reasoned that his mother would know that, and hoped if she did note the lack of outward affection between them, Mrs Hemming would put it down to the fact that both her son and his fiancée were rather 'private people'.

Having sorted this out to her satisfaction, Lucy felt the first stirrings of interest in her weekend away from Brook House. At the beginning of the journey Mrs Hemming had enthused about Malvern, telling Lucy of the pleasures it had to offer besides the hills that Edward Elgar had once trodden and probably gained his inspiration to write some of his superb music.

Lost in her own thoughts, Lucy was brought back to the present by Jud's easy, 'Nearly there,' as the Bentley effortlessly began to climb. 'I expect you could do with stretching your legs—we'll take a walk after you've had a cup of tea.'

There was no 'Would you like to take a walk?', just a plain statement of fact. But as the car carried on its upward climb, Lucy found the niggle of irritation she had expected to feel at his pronouncement of what they would do unexpectedly missing. Perhaps a walk—she expected it would be on the hills—was just what she would like, though she was uncertain that Jud was the companion she would have chosen.

Mrs Hemming stirred just as Jud pulled on to the short drive outside a house that was about the same size as Brook House, though not as old. Built at the turn of the century, Lucy thought, as she stepped out of the car and looked to the front door where a plump woman had come out to join them as Jud helped his mother from the car.

'I've been looking out for you,' the plump woman said, coming up to them. 'The kettle is on the boil all ready.'

She was a friendly woman and appeared to have a great affection for Mrs Hemming and Jud, and Lucy learned on being introduced to Lottie that she had been with Mrs Hemming 'for years', and when Mrs Hemming had moved to Malvern, there had been no question but that Lottie should come too.

Jud had them all ushered inside the house with the minimum amount of fuss. 'I'll take the cases up while you talk to Lottie,' he told his mother, and then turning to Lucy who had stood inside the pleasant sitting room while Lottie had enquired first as to Mrs Hemming's health, then shrieked with pleasure on learning that Jud was engaged, he said, 'Come with me, Lucy, I'll show you your room.'

Lucy went with him up the staircase thickly carpeted in red and held in place by shining brass stair rods. Her room was to the left of the landing which had a few more doors going to either side of the door he opened for her. Expecting Jud to just drop her case and depart, she was mildly surprised when he came into the room with her and after depositing her suitcase on the warm pink carpet he went over to the window. He seemed to find the view very satisfying and, unconscious that she had moved, Lucy went to join him.

'Why, it's beautiful!' was drawn from her as she looked

at the view that stretched for miles and miles.

She stood enraptured looking down over Herefordshire and gazed her fill, unspeaking, until Jud turned from the window. 'Mother particularly wanted you to have this room because of the view,' he told her quietly, adding, 'She likes you, Lucy.'

Lucy stared at him; for all his face was unsmiling the grey-green eyes she had thought so cold had an unexpected warmth in them, and she looked hurriedly away as a mixture of feelings within her fought for precedence. The feeling of guilt at the way they were deceiving Mrs Hemming won over the surprising, almost earth-shaking feeling that he might be very nice if the warmth in his eyes ever stayed there for any length of time.

'That doesn't make me feel any better about what we're doing,' she said flatly, wishing he would tell his mother about Carol and the need for this charade. She looked at him again to find that cold look had returned to his eyes.

'Needs must when the devil drives,' he said, which left her knowing Carol was the particular devil in this case. Jud walked over to the door. 'Try to strangle that conscience of yours this weekend,' he instructed. 'My mother wants you to enjoy yourself. Tea will be ready in a few minutes.' With that he left her.

Lucy was glad to be on her own. She went over to the window as if hoping the calming view would quieten the upsurge of emotions that had beset her when Jud had been in the room.

He would be taking her back on Sunday, and until then she had to behave as if she hung on his every word. Strangle her conscience, he had said, but that was easier said than done, and if he wasn't such an insensitive brute he would realise that. But no, that was too much to hope for; all he was concerned with was that the hold Carol Stanfield had on him must be broken. Lucy spent a few minutes wondering about his relationship with Carol, then feeling an emotion she didn't recognise, only knowing she didn't like it—that churning up feeling inside her—she went into the bathroom that led off her bedroom, washed her hands, ran a comb through her hair, and thought it about time she joined the others downstairs. She would unpack the few things she had brought with her later.

Since they would be dining at eight, tea was a light affair with Mrs Hemming presiding over the teapot. 'Lucy and I thought we'd go for a walk,' Jud announced, having downed two cups of tea, and now looking ready for some action.

'You're never still two minutes,' his mother scolded him fondly. 'Still, I expect Lucy would like to have a look round, and I must telephone Vera Stanfield.'

Lucy managed to smile as she stood up to accompany Jud out of the room, but her mind was racing with thoughts of *who was Vera Stanfield*? Was she related to Carol? And if so, what would Vera Stanfield think of Jud becoming engaged so soon after Carol had left the Hall, for Carol had been nowhere in evidence when she had dined at the Hall the day Jud had given her her ring.

Her thoughts too chaotic to think of anything other than the problem immediately on her mind, Lucy set out for her walk with Jud without giving heed to the thought that she would be better equipped for walking in the flat-heeled shoes that were now in her case.

They crossed the road after leaving the house and were at once at the foot of several pathways that led to the crown of one of the range of hills. 'We'll keep to this path,' Jud told her, leading her away from a well trodden grassy path and along the hardened surface of a constructed pathway. 'You'll find it hard going in those shoes on the other path,' he said, noticing where she had not that two-inch heels were not quite the thing for scrambling up a grassy incline.

'Who is Vera Stanfield?' Lucy asked bluntly, her footwear the least of her worries at that moment.

There was a silence that stretched between them for so long that she thought Jud wasn't going to answer her, then he said, 'Vera Stanfield is Carol Stanfield's mother.'

'Carol's mother?' she questioned, startled. She wanted to know more, much more, but she doubted Jud would tell her anything he didn't think it necessary for her to know.

But to her surprise Jud gave in to her obvious mystification. 'Vera Stanfield and my mother have known each other for years—they were at school together. They married round about the same time and what one did the other seemed to do too. They're very close friends,' he informed her, 'and share each other's joys and woes. When I arrived Vera Stanfield was very upset, so I believe, that she wasn't able to produce offspring too—but that's the way it goes, and sad though it is, after ten barren years Vera and her husband adopted a baby.'

'Carol,' Lucy put in, her confused thoughts temporarily ousted by a feeling of instant sympathy for the unknown Vera Stanfield who had so yearned for a baby.

'Carol,' Jud confirmed. 'And what a delight she turned out to be.'

Some of Lucy's sympathy ebbed at the warm note in Jud's voice. Surely he hadn't ... She tried to blank the thought off, but it persisted—the thought that left a nasty taste in her mouth that Jud had betrayed the trust Mrs Stanfield must have in him, the thought that he had taken her daughter ...

'Before your mind becomes tangled up in mucky imaginings,' Jud broke into her thoughts coldly, 'I'll tell you now that Carol and I have never had an affair.'

Lucy had no answer to that. Furious she might be that he had read her mind so accurately, but she wouldn't forgive him for that 'mucky imaginings'. What else was she to think—the girl had been wearing her ring, and all the information she had had prior to his sudden announcement to the contrary had led her to believe Carol had indeed shared his bed at some time or another.

Since his remark had successfully silenced her, Jud went on: 'I've said Carol is a delight, and so she is—a bit scatterbrained maybe, but a delightful child nonetheless.'

Lucy did some quick mental arithmetic. Jud had told her he was thirty-five, so if Carol had arrived ten years after him, then Carol must be twenty-five. A delightful child, he had said—Carol was three years older than she was. Lucy remembered the girl with the friendly smile and realised then that probably since Jud had known Carol from the time she had been an infant, she would always appear to him to be no more than a child.

They walked on, neither saying anything as Lucy tried to sort out her confused thoughts. A picture of her brother flashed through her mind. Rupert was the same age as Carol—a man in his own right—but she never thought of him as that, he was just the brother she had grown up with; perhaps that was how Jud regarded Carol. Lucy found the oddest pleasure in that thought and didn't know why. She shrugged thoughts of Rupert away and returned to the subject Jud must have thought finished with—there were still one or two questions that needed to be cleared up, and she considered that even as his mock-fiancée, she was entitled to have a few answers.

CHAPTER FIVE

HER feet firmly rooted to the ground, Lucy came to a standstill. The more she thought about her mock engagement the more confused she became, and suddenly she wasn't going to go another step until Jud had told her what she wanted to know. They hadn't been walking fast, just strolling up the sloping path. Jud must have been miles away with his own thoughts, but when he realised she was no longer with him he retraced his steps and came back to join her, a look of mild enquiry on his face.

'Would you mind, Jud Hemming, telling me what exactly I'm doing being *engaged* to you?'

'I thought you knew.' His tone was as mild as his look, but that didn't put her off. She knew if there was anything devious going on—and the thought that it was was growing larger by the minute—then she knew his quick-thinking brain would be doing some rapid calculations behind that bland mask.

'That's just it—I don't know,' she said, a determined look on her face.

Jud looked at her briefly, then turned to a bench nearby where the not-so-fit could take a breather before going on, and led her over to it. When they were both sitting down he glanced her way again, but Lucy didn't wait for whatever clever remark he had thought up to flatten her with, but plunged straight in.

'I agreed to this farce because I believed that by showing you were engaged to me you would be extracting yourself from a very clinging female who couldn't see your affair was finished, and also in order to reclaim a ring that's rightfully mine anyway,' she told him, stating the facts as she

78

saw them, pausing only when it looked as though Jud was going to insert something. She gave him a hasty glance, but he looked quite imperturbable and had nothing to say, it seemed, except an extremely polite:

'Do carry on.'

Lucy had no need of further invitation. 'I thought it was a straightforward deal between the two of us—naturally I felt sorry for Carol ...'

'Naturally,' he put in.

Lucy ignored him. 'I thought no one need know but the three of us ...'

'You reckoned without your brother.'

That was below the belt, Lucy considered, but having got so far she was determined not to be put off. 'Yes, well——' she said, barely hesitating, 'That's beside the point.' She knew it wasn't, if Rupert had been able to keep the information to himself she wouldn't be here now. 'Now you tell me that you and Carol have never—never ...'

'If you're looking for the correct term, try "Gone to bed with each other",' Jud inserted mockingly.

'Well, if you haven't—and by the sound of it you regard Carol as no more than you would a sister—then would you mind telling me what I'm doing playing the part of your fiancée?' Lucy came to a storming, heated finish and glared at him as she thought she detected a slight twitching at the corner of his mouth.

When he looked at her stern-faced, she knew she had mistaken that anything she had said had remotely amused him. 'You're right, my feelings for Carol are those of an elder brother, and perhaps I did give you the wrong idea about her and me—but,' he added quite calmly, 'it was you who took it for granted she was my fiancée when you came to the Hall that night—I never once claimed a relationship of that sort with her.'

Lucy tried to think back to what exactly had been said, and found she was too worked up to remember clearly. Yes, she had thought him engaged to Carol, had probably said as much, but . . . 'All right, I'll give you that,' she had to allow. 'But if Carol wasn't interested in you—that way—that still doesn't explain this.' She thrust her hand with the ring firmly on her engagement finger in front of him.

'There you have it,' he said obscurely.

'What . . .?' Lucy asked shortly, and found herself unanswered as Jud left her to work it out for herself. 'There you have it', he'd said. What did she have? Lucy backtracked over their conversation.

Jud had said he and Carol had not slept together, that he thought of Carol as he might a sister—Lucy puzzled away and could make nothing of what had been said to make it necessary for Jud to appear to be engaged until, about to ask him to explain, he looked at her and, reluctantly it seemed, told her what her confused brain refused to work out.

'You remarked, I believe, "but if Carol isn't interested in you in that way".'

And then Lucy had it. 'Oh,' she said, and couldn't for the moment think of anything smarter than that to say. 'You mean that while your feelings for Carol are not romantically inclined—she, without any assistance from you, thinks herself in love with you.'

'I'm afraid so,' Jud said slowly, then opening up, 'I've told her flatly she's wasting her time.' Lucy could just imagine how cruel Jud would be in putting that across, and winced for the poor girl. 'But the young minx came back with "Where there's life there's hope".'

'So to stop Carol thinking there was a chance with you, you told her you were engaged.' Lucy spoke her thoughts aloud. She couldn't help feeling sorry for the girl who had left the Hall straightaway and gone to lick her wounds in private. 'But how did she come to be wearing my ring? Did you just leave it lying around and . . .'

'You must think me very careless,' Jud broke in

smoothly, and went on to tell her, 'Originally I bought the
ring for my mother's birthday next month—she's very fond
of antique jewellery,' Lucy winced to think she had de-
prived Jud's mother of something she would have loved.
'Not to worry,' Jud said on seeing her expression, 'I shall
look around for something she'll like equally well.' He
watched as Lucy's face cleared then went on, 'When I
examined the ring I thought one of the stones wasn't as
secure as it might have been, so I left it with a London firm
of jewellers to have it checked over—Carol arranged to
come and stay while my mother was at the Hall and since
I hadn't any immediate plans to go to London I sent Carol
the jewellers' receipt and asked her to collect the ring and
bring it with her when she came. She arrived late on Sunday night and gave me the ring after my mother had gone
to bed the following evening.'

'And in the meantime you'd been to the village hall and
I'd seen my ring on Carol's finger when she came into the
cloakroom,' Lucy inserted.

Jud inclined his head in agreement. 'Carol must have
been overtaken by some imp of mischief and put it on in
between going to collect my mother's wrap and meeting us
back at the door—she certainly didn't have it on when she
joined us.'

He had explained everything very smoothly, re-affirmed
that the sole reason for their engagement was to stop Carol
from thinking she would ever become Mrs Judson Hemming, and Lucy felt a little foolish for having brought the
subject up at all when it was only slightly different from the
original reason for the engagement anyway—the difference
being that whereas before she had thought Carol was a girl-
friend Jud had grown tired of and was using the engagement as a means of getting rid of her, she now knew he had
never had an affair with the girl and that his action in getting engaged had been purely to try and stop Carol thinking romantically about him. Carol might be hurt for a

while, Lucy mused, but wasn't Jud right? Wasn't it better, with Jud's feelings for her being those of a brother, that she should discover now she was wasting her time rather than spend her youth in hoping for something that could never be?

Feeling uneasy that Jud wasn't the villain she had been so ready to believe he was, Lucy got up from the bench and, unable to look at him, found he had followed suit and was turning her back the way they had come.

Dinner that evening passed without mishap. Lucy had showered and changed into a pale green kaftan with darker green embroidery picked out on all the hemlines. She saw Jud's glance flick over her when she joined him and Mrs Hemming for a pre-dinner drink and knew she was looking good, but for all she could read from his expression she might just as well be dressed in a piece of old sacking.

Talk over the meal was fairly general, though at one stage Jud thought to hope his mother had found Mrs Stanfield well when she had telephoned her.

'Yes, she's fine. Carol had nipped off to Tenerife—such a lively child,' she explained, turning to Lucy. 'I expect Jud has told you about Vera and Carol?'

'Yes, he has,' Lucy smiled back, and refused to look in Jud's direction.

'Carol came to stay at the Hall over the Bank Holiday,' Mrs Hemming went on, 'but like the butterfly creature she is, she didn't stay long.'

It was obvious that Mrs Hemming had a deep affection for Carol and with the indulgence of long acquaintance, could see nothing wrong in the fact that Carol had suddenly taken it into her head to leave the Hall after so brief a stay. Lucy sincerely hoped the other girl was beginning to get over her hurt.

Mrs Hemming decided to go to bed shortly after the meal, and Lucy thought she would follow suit—the last thing she wanted was to be left alone with Jud. She stirred in her seat, aware that Jud's eyes were on her, but before she could voice her intention to go to bed too, she heard Jud saying teasingly:

'I don't know whether you're truly tired, Mother, or just being tactful.'

'I am tired, Jud,' Mrs Hemming said severely, but Lucy could see a twinkle in her eye that belied the sternness, and thought fleetingly, why, she's very like Jud when she looks like that, though for the life of her she couldn't ever remember Jud's eyes twinkling. 'I was young and in love myself once,' Mrs Hemming recalled, a gentle expression ousting all severity. 'I don't suppose you will mind being left alone with each other.'

After that, it was impossible for Lucy to carry out her intention of going to bed, and after Mrs Hemming had left she subsided back in her chair wondering how long she would have to sit it out before she could make her escape. She wondered what, if anything, she and Jud would find to talk about which wouldn't end up with her on the receiving end of his stinging sarcasm, for she doubted that such a cold man as she knew him to be would put himself out to be pleasant now there would be no one there to act as witness.

After handing her a glass of gin and tonic, Jud took the chair facing her. 'Is your drink to your liking?' he enquired —she had asked for more tonic water than gin.

Lucy took a sip and told him it was, 'Just right, thanks,' then searched round in her mind for some subject of conversation that might get her through the next hour. 'Do you often go to Germany?' she asked, that question being the best she could come up with, and if Jud realised she was bent on being the perfect guest, there was nothing in his face to show it amused him.

'I visit various parts of the globe in my business,' he told her, letting her know his trip had not been purely for pleasure, and matching his mood to hers, which surprised her, went on to tell her, in the manner of a perfect host, about the various countries he had been to, drawing from her the admission that she had been to some of those places herself.

Lucy found his conversation interesting. Not once had either of them said a word that would get the other to fire back, and it was with wonder that on flicking a glance to her wrist when a break in the conversation occurred, that she saw it was half past eleven.

'Good heavens!' she exclaimed, having thought the hands might be creeping round to half past ten and that there would only be another half an hour to go before she could decently make her escape, 'it's half past eleven.' As she spoke she stood up.

'It wasn't nearly as bad as you thought it was going to be, was it?' Jud said smoothly, as he rose to his feet and came to stand looking down into her dark brown eyes.

So he knew she had been on edge at the thought of having to spend an hour solely in his company. 'You can be fairly tolerable when you make the effort,' she came back coolly, letting him know she had been aware that while a guest in his mother's house they had both been on their best behaviour.

She saw his lips twitch at her remark, and without wanting to, found her own mouth turning up at the corners as she looked up at him. She saw his glance go to her mouth, and watched while all amusement went from his face.

'I think it's time you were in bed,' he observed abruptly, giving her a tight look and turning away. 'You seem to be very slightly at risk.'

'At risk?' she queried, feeling a sudden tingle in her veins at the tenseness that had so quickly come between them. What had his look meant—did he mean she ran the risk of being kissed? She stayed where she was when all reason told her she should go.

Jud turned to face her, his face once more expressionless.

'You're in danger of letting that acid little tongue of yours have its way,' he supplied calmly.

Lucy wasn't quite sure how she got out of the room, was aware of giving him a quietly spoken, terse, 'Goodnight,' which wasn't answered, had no recollection of negotiating the stairs, and only came to life when realising she was automatically preparing for bed. She felt oddly let down, disappointed even, which was ridiculous. She hadn't wanted him to kiss her, had she, for goodness' sake? Of course she hadn't—why, the very idea was preposterous! Just because she'd spent a pleasant hour and a half with him ... Pleasant? Well yes, she supposed it had been pleasant, she admitted grudgingly; the time had sped quickly by anyhow. But she had had other such evenings with many people and had never thought to be kissed at the end of it. Perhaps she'd had too much to drink, was her next thought, only she knew she hadn't, for when Jud had offered to refill her glass she had declined, and you really couldn't lose your sense of proportion on one small gin and a lot of tonic, could you?

When Lucy got up the next morning she was able to scoff at her imaginings of the night before. Honestly, she mused, she must have been knocked off balance by the fact that Jud had bothered to play host at all with no one around to see.

Jud had already gone out, she was informed by Lottie when she joined the housekeeper in the kitchen. It was still early yet and Mrs Hemming wasn't down. 'I'd like her to stay in bed for as long as she will,' Lottie told Lucy, and went on to explain that it had recently been discovered that Mrs Hemming had a slight heart complaint. 'Nothing too serious,' Lottie told her. 'It was only discovered when she went down with an attack of 'flu. Jud has been on at her ever since to move into a bungalow—he's not at all happy about her climbing the stairs, but Mrs Hemming can be as stubborn as Jud when she makes up her mind to anything.'

Lucy's thoughts were still with Mrs Hemming and her slight heart condition, when Lottie said if she would like to go into the dining room she would bring her breakfast to her, and mindful of the extra work Lottie would have with her and Jud staying for the weekend, Lucy straightaway offered to make her own breakfast and asked could she eat it in the kitchen.

'Why bless you, of course you can,' said Lottie, and opined that Jud had got himself engaged to a real little lady.

Not knowing quite what to say in answer to Lottie's compliment, but experiencing a stab of guilt that here was another dear soul she and Jud were deceiving, Lucy went over to the cooker and was just asking, 'Has Jud had his breakfast?' when the kitchen door opened.

'No, he hasn't,' Jud said from the doorway. 'If you're on kitchen fatigues this morning can I have my bacon crisp?'

Lucy was glad of Lottie's presence as she and Jud sat in the kitchen eating their breakfast. Having no fancy to be alone with him, she had been dreading the whole time the bacon had been sizzling in the pan that Lottie would insist that they should eat in the dining room now that Jud was there, but Lottie didn't, and refused Lucy's offer to cook her something, saying she had already eaten, though when pressed by Jud she did sit down with them and shared the coffee pot with them.

'Fancy a walk to the top of the Beacon after lunch?' Jud asked Lucy, telling her, 'I've got one or two jobs lined up for me this morning.'

'The Beacon? Isn't that the highest of the hills?' Hadn't Mrs Hemming said that yesterday in the car?

Lottie joined in the conversation, confirming Lucy's question, and adding, 'I've never been to the top myself, but they do say on a clear day you can see miles—even as far as the Bristol Channel.' It was easy to see, as Lottie warmed to her theme, that she had taken Malvern to her heart since she had moved there with Mrs Hemming. 'No end of famous people used to live in or around Malvern,' she told Lucy while Jud looked on. Elizabeth Barrett, the poet, had lived at Hope End, Lucy learned. Jenny Lind, the Swedish soprano, had lived at Wynds Point where she had died at the age of sixty-seven and was now buried in Malvern, her husband following her to rest twenty years later. And carrying on from there Lottie told an interested Lucy that Peter Roget was buried in West Malvern, though Lottie said she didn't know very much about him. Lucy thought she must mean Peter Roget of *Thesaurus* fame, and listened to learn what else Lottie had to say until Lottie said, 'Well, this is no good—I must get on.'

'Lucy and I will wash up if you want to get on with something else,' Jud told her, coming into the conversation for the first time, having seemed quite content to sit back and watch Lucy and his mother's help getting to know each other. 'Knowing you, you'll want all the cushions plumped up before I take you into town.'

Lucy got up from the table as Lottie, with a duster in her overall pocket, left the room. 'I could have offered to do the dusting,' she said, in half a mind to follow Lottie and tell her so—she could be doing that while Lottie and Jud were in town.

Jud caught hold of Lucy's arm and pulled her round to face him. 'There's no need,' he said. 'I suspect you're kept busy at Brook House—have a rest this weekend.' Lucy looked up and witnessed the not so cold look in his eyes that she had seen there once before. 'You have a nice way with you, Lucy,' he added quietly and unexpectedly, and not knowing what to make of that, especially as once again his eyes dropped to her mouth and back again and she had already established satisfactorily to herself that he had no desire to kiss her, Lucy looked away.

Feeling strangely restless, she began clearing the table and found Jud helping her while she was still trying to sort out what, if anything, he had meant by 'You have a nice way with you'. The only conclusion she could come to as she rinsed through the dishes they had used, watching Jud from the corner of her eye as he picked up a cloth and began to dry them, was that he must mean the easy way she and Lottie had got on with each other. Then came another disquieting thought ...

'I wasn't being nice to Lottie for my own ends,' she blurted out without thinking.

'Own ends?' Jud queried, clearly having no idea what she was talking about.

Lucy wished then that she had thought before she said anything. It was too late now and Jud was obviously waiting for her to explain her statement.

'Well, I know you haven't any great opinion of women,' and me in particular, she almost added, but that was getting away from the point. 'But in case you're thinking I was trying to get round Lottie and through her your mother, and through your mother to you—I wasn't.' She wished she had never got started on this, for Jud was looking at her blankly as if trying to fathom what on earth she was talking about. Bravely she carried on, though was aware her creamy complexion was tinged with a pink glow. 'When we had help at Brook House——' she began again, and bit her lip before remembering that Jud already knew she and Rupert no longer employed outside help, so she hadn't let slip anything he wasn't aware of, 'Well, our help then was always treated as part of the family,' she added, and concentrated her attention on the rose-patterned cup in her hand.

'That rose won't scrub off,' Jud said behind her, drawing her attention to the fact she must have been rubbing away at it for at least a minute. She felt something touch the top of her head, and because her hands were awash with soapy water, flicked her head instinctively while the shattering thought came to her that Jud had just kissed the top of her head. Her imagination was having a field day, she realised, as Jud came to take up his position once more, having deposited the dried-up articles on the kitchen table.

'What you're trying to say, I think, is that you like talking to Lottie purely because she's Lottie. That you fancy neither my bank balance nor me—in other words, what you're trying to say in the politest way possible is that Jud Hemming doesn't turn Lucy Carey on, is that right?'

His voice didn't sound as though that last thought bothered him in the slightest, and Lucy was sure it didn't bother her one iota that he was indifferent to her not fancying him.

'I couldn't have put it better if I'd spent all day working on it,' she told him coolly, without realising her confirming words might by some men have been taken as a challenge for them to try and get her to alter her opinion.

Though Jud retained his offhand manner, his voice was a shade harder as he informed her, 'If it means anything to you, I long ago took you out of the same category as some of my more hardened female acquaintances.'

Lucy wished Lottie would come back soon. Surprise at his comment had very nearly made her drop the saucer she was holding. She took refuge in a short, sharp, sarcastic comment.

'I'm honoured.'

She half turned as Lottie came into the kitchen and caught an expression on Jud's face that made her stomach turn over, for there was no mistaking his look; it said as clearly as if he had spoken that she was going to have to pay for her sarcasm.

Mrs Hemming appeared shortly before Jud and Lottie went out to the car ready to go into town, and while Lottie was asking Mrs Hemming if there was anything she could get her while she was out, Jud turned to Lucy and said quietly, 'I'll be back as soon as I can.' Which was considerate of him, she thought when he had gone, because she had to own she was not a little anxious in case Mrs Hemming asked her something that required an outright lie. Jud, she knew, would have been equal to avoiding giving a direct answer, but Lucy knew she would be out of her depth when trying to avoid lying to this woman whose gentle ways reminded her so much of her own mother.

'You don't mind that Jud has had to leave you for a short while, Lucy?' Mrs Hemming asked as they sat in the sitting room with a tray of coffee between them on a small occasional table. 'Neither Lottie nor I drive and the bus service isn't brilliant, and although we have most things delivered, items like tapestry wool and the like do mean a journey into town. When I've gone with Lottie before we usually go by taxi, but with Jud here with the car ...'

'I don't mind a bit,' Lucy said quickly, then thinking it might sound to Mrs Hemming as though she couldn't wait for Jud to be gone, added, 'We're taking a walk to the top of the Beacon this afternoon.'

Mrs Hemming smiled back, interested. 'It's a long way up,' she said, having noticed nothing in Lucy's manner to suggest that Jud could stay out for the rest of the day as far as she was concerned. 'There's a café at the top, I believe—you'll be able to have a cup of tea when you get there—though I don't suppose either of you will notice the climb.'

Lucy took a sip of her coffee and avoided answering, not being sure if Jud's mother was meaning that their younger limbs would make nothing of the climb or that she believed them to be so much in love they could climb Everest and not notice the pull.

True to his word Jud was back with Lottie in just over an hour, and during the time spent alone with Mrs Hemming Lucy had not had recourse to summon up the whitest of lies, since with Mrs Hemming, believing she wanted to know all there was to know about Jud, had regaled her with snippets from happenings when he was at school, then university, to the small industrial plant he had inherited from his father, to the way he had worked day and night to make the company the big concern it now was.

After lunch Mrs Hemming went to her room to rest, and at Jud's enquiry of, 'Did you think to bring some flat shoes?' Lucy went to her room, changing not only her shoes for a pair of lightweight walking shoes, but slipping off her dress and donning a pair of white jeans and a red short sleeved collarless shirt. It was a warm day and she thought she might well be overheated when they reached their destination, but if, as she suspected he would, Jud decided to ignore the constructed path and elected the way to the top of the Beacon by way of the grassy inclines, then she felt jeans would be more decorous for anything she might meet.

Jud himself was dressed in lightweight slacks and a loose-fitting sports shirt when she joined him, but she needn't have worried about their route, for although as she suspected they took the well trodden paths over the grass, she did not have to do any energy-sapping scrambling as she observed one or two teenagers were doing as they ignored the more sedate paths and scrambled up the hill-side that was very steep in parts.

'Too hot for that sort of caper,' Jud remarked, seeing her eyes on the teenagers who were shrieking with laughter as one of their members slipped and rolled back several yards. Lucy was inclined to agree with him, though she couldn't help feeling slightly wistful at the completely un-inhibited way the teenagers were spending their afternoon.

'I don't suppose you've ever frolicked in your life,' she said, her mind still on the group.

'Now what I wonder makes you think that,' Jud said easily.

'Well,' Lucy replied, wishing for the umpteenth time she had bothered to think before she spoke, 'you always appear so cold and formal.'

'Do I?' Jud sounded surprised, then, 'Are you advocating that I lose some of my formality with you?'

'No—oh no, of course not,' she answered quickly, looking away from what she suspected was a gleam of devilment in his eyes.

Fortunately at that moment they reached a crest in the hills where a marker showed many directions, and Lucy went over to study it. There were two routes showing the way to the Beacon, she saw, and she read with her mind barely on what she was reading, being more full of the devilment she thought she had seen in Jud's eyes. She forced herself to concentrate on another arrow that pointed out Sugar Loaf, and very conscious of Jud's nearness behind her as he looked over her shoulder, she moved round until Jud was opposite her, a feeling of disquiet motivating her feet, and studied the pointer that said Horse Shoe Bend, and began to feel better when Jud didn't move to come to her side. She looked at him then, the rock-made marker between them, and as their eyes caught and held, she wanted to make some trite remark—Jud was wearing that enigmatic expression again, but there was nothing cold or formal about the look in his eyes.

'You know, Lucy,' he said smoothly, and she felt herself unable to look away from him, 'you've made one or two challenging remarks today—might I suggest that if you're going to get cold feet at the last moment, you think twice before you speak?'

She did manage to look away from him then. She knew her cheeks were pink from the implied threat behind his words, and she hoped he would think her high colour was on account of her exertions so far, rather than from the thought of what he would do if she issued one more challenging remark. Without saying another word she walked away from the marker and found Jud beside her as they began the steeper climb.

Surely Jud wasn't bothered that he didn't 'turn her on',

she mused, as the ascent became steeper still. Of course he wasn't—she dismissed the idea as ludicrous. And she hadn't thought her 'I'm honoured' this morning had been all that challenging either—sarcastic, yes, but she recalled at the time that Jud's look had said she was going to pay for her sarcasm. She shouldn't have told him she saw him as cold and formal, though ...

They reached their destination and paused in silence to take in the view before them. Although they had seen several people with the same quest in mind, they seemed to have the hills entirely to themselves just then. The view was splendid, but Lucy was overwhelmingly conscious of Jud by her side, especially when his arm came about her shoulder and he turned her to show her another aspect of the view before them. Her heart was beating erratically inside her; she was certain this was because of the effort involved in the climb—what else could it possibly be? The feel of Jud's arm across her shoulders had nothing at all to do with it, though she wished he was still as she had described him, cold and formal; that way he would merely have said 'look over there', the need to turn her to show her unnecessary.

'Tea?'

'What?' So deep in her own thoughts had she been, she wasn't with him.

'I said would you like a cup of tea?'

'Yes—thank you.'

Jud's arm dropped away from her shoulders as they turned their backs on the view and he pointed out another marker that proclaimed 'Worcestershire Beacon. The highest point of the Malverns 1395 ft.', before he placed his hand beneath her elbow and guided her through a cutting to the café.

The café was full, but there were benches and tables outside, and Lucy sat in the sunshine waiting for Jud to bring the tea, very much of the opinion that she would be glad when she returned to Brook House. As she had suspected she was finding this weekend upsetting—but not as she had thought because of her fear of betraying the true state of affairs between her and Jud to his mother, but because Jud was proving to have the most upsetting effect on her equilibrium.

The walk down the hill was completed much more quickly and almost without conversation. On her part Lucy was afraid of making any comment that could be construed in any way as challenging, and Jud seemed to have thoughts of his own to keep him occupied.

The rest of Saturday passed without incident. But where Lucy had set out by wanting to avoid being left alone with Mrs Hemming lest she gave something away without thinking, she now found herself anxious to avoid being alone with Jud. So much so that when at ten o'clock Mrs Hemming said she was going to bed, regardless of what she might think, knowing only that she couldn't face being left alone with Jud, Lucy stood up too.

'I think I'll go to bed myself if no one minds,' she said quietly, and as both Jud and Mrs Hemming looked at her —Mrs Hemming with faint surprise in her look, Jud giving her a look that if she knew him better she might have thought said 'coward'—she added, 'That climb up the hill— all that fresh air ...'' her voice tailed off as Mrs Hemming's surprise turned to understanding.

'Shall I come and tuck you up?' Jud asked outrageously.

'Jud!' his mother said sharply, which had little effect on him other than to produce a most definite grin as he studied both his mother's and Lucy's shocked faces.

Lucy had wild thoughts of putting a chair beneath the door handle of her room when the door was firmly closed and she was alone, then she realised that wouldn't be necessary. Jud's 'Shall I come and tuck you up?' had been said merely to jolt her, and she hadn't been quick enough to disguise the fact that his aim had been achieved.

CHAPTER SIX

LUCY awoke the next morning glad she would be going home that day. She hadn't slept very well, with thoughts of Jud Hemming too much at the forefront of her mind to make sleep easy to come by.

Something had been said yesterday about her and Jud leaving some time after lunch—she wished the hours quickly to roll by so that she could once again be at Brook House with her brother.

Poor Rupert, she had given him very little thought over this weekend, and it wasn't that she was so uncaring either —it was just that Jud Hemming was so vital somehow that being in the same house with him seemed to have eclipsed thoughts and worries about the one person in the world she was close to.

Lucy regretted that she couldn't be completely herself with Mrs Hemming, but never knowing what Jud's mother might say next that might require an evasive answer, Lucy knew she had at times been far from natural with her— though she was glad to think that since Mrs Hemming didn't know her very well, she wouldn't have noticed anything amiss and if she had seen she was hesitant from time to time she would, in all likelihood, put it down to a quirk in her personality.

The morning passed with Jud driving them all to church and then he had a look at the washing machine which Lottie said was 'playing up', but not so badly that it required an engineer to be called out to take a look at it. Lunch of roast beef with all the trimmings passed off with no awkward moments for Lucy, and when Jud said as the three of them sat in the sitting room afterwards, 'We'll get

off in about an hour, Lucy,' her relief had her on her feet
to go and pack her few things together.

Quite what made her change into the ice blue linen two-
piece she had worn to travel in on Friday she wasn't sure,
but instead of packing it away once she had taken it from
the wardrobe, she laid it on the bed instead, then pulling
the dress she was wearing over her head, she popped that
inside her case and stepped inside the bathroom to have a
quick wash.

She was just zipping up her skirt, the top still reposing
on the bed, when her bedroom door opened and without
so much as a 'by your leave' Jud strolled in.

A gasp of pure amazement left Lucy to see him there,
taking completely out of her head for a split moment that
while the bottom half of her was decently clad, Jud had
full view of her bare arm and the rest of her top covered in
a fine lacy petticoat. She saw from his look that he appreciated what he could see.

'I ... d ... Get out!' she spluttered, jerking the matching
top to her skirt off the bed and holding it in front of her.
Jud had left the door standing wide open, but nevertheless
he was blocking the doorway, giving her the oppressive,
breath-halting feeling that the door was solidly shut with no
way out.

'Such modesty,' he said lightly, and advanced further
into the room. Lucy tried to back away from him, but the
solid bed was against her legs and she could go no further.

'Y—You have no business in here,' she said heatedly,
hugging the top to her and wishing it possible to get into
her jacket without revealing her front—she wasn't going to
turn her back on him.

'Oh, but I have,' he said, coming another step nearer.

Lucy's eyes widened in alarm. Oh God, he was scaring
her—was he now about to exact retribution for those unthinking remarks he had taken as challenging? She felt
herself go pale at the thought, then to her further astonish-

ment, Jud stopped where he was. Two feet away was too
close, Lucy thought—then he opened his mouth and
laughed as if he thought the sight of her half dressed, with
her fear naked for him to see, amusing.

'Oh, lord, Lucy,' he grinned, when his mirth had died
away. 'You look as though you fear a fate worse than death!'

Lucy felt the colour return to her cheeks; so he hadn't
got that in mind. 'I have told you before I'm unused to having men in my room,' she said chokingly, refusing to allow
the tight grip she had on the ice blue shield in front of her
slacken.

'You don't know what you're missing,' Jud told her. He
could be quite monstrous when he chose, she thought with
one corner of her mind, while the rest of her watched him
as though still not convinced she could trust him. 'Oh, put
that thing on,' Jud said irritably. 'You haven't got anything
I haven't seen before.'

Oh, if only she had her hands free, Lucy thought, still
refusing to let go of the top, she'd make his ears sing for
him. 'If you have something constructive to say,' she told
him coldly, 'just say it and get out.' She knew from the way
his eyes narrowed that he didn't like her tone, but she refused to let her eyes drop.

'Very well,' he said after a few moments of tense silence.
'I've just been having a word with my mother—or rather,'
he amended, 'my mother has been having a word with me.
It seems you and I have not been playing the role of an
engaged couple the way we should.' Lucy's mouth opened,
then was firmly closed again as she waited for him to continue. 'A few things haven't escaped her notice this weekend,' he went on, 'and though she's aware that I'm not
openly demonstrative she's left wondering if you're happy
—my mother is very concerned about you, Lucy.'

The last thing Lucy wanted was for Mrs Hemming to
worry about her, particularly since she was now acquainted

with the fact that Jud's mother had a slight heart condition.

'Wh—what sort of things haven't escaped her notice?' she asked, realising now it had perhaps been necessary for Jud to come to her room if he wanted a word with her where there was no chance of them being overheard— though they would be going home shortly ...

'Things like the way you and I never touch each other for a start,' Jud said. 'Apparently it's the done thing for people in love to touch each other now and then—My mother noticed when you went to bed last night that although you kissed her cheek, I got nothing.'

'Oh!'

'Yes, Lucy—oh.'

'I never thought,' Lucy faltered, and knew even if she had, if Jud had proffered his cheek the way his mother had done last night, she would have pretended not to see it.

Jud ignored her comment and went on to tell her what he proposed they should do. 'I've said that we had a lovers' tiff when we were out yesterday,' he told her, 'but that we've enjoyed making up and now everything is fine. We now have less than an hour in which to convince her that we're in love and sublimely happy in each other's company.'

That good an actress Lucy knew she was not. 'You're not proposing I come downstairs and fling myself in your arms, I trust?' She took refuge in sarcasm as the very idea set up a fluttery sensation in her stomach. Flinging herself into Jud's arms wouldn't have convinced Mrs Hemming anyway, she would know by now that, like her son, she wasn't demonstrative in public.

'Others have done it without feeling any after-effects,' Jud said coolly, his eyes watching the expressions flitting across her face.

'Like you, Jud, I'm choosey,' Lucy said recklessly, while thinking if she wasn't careful she was going to end up paying for her sarcasm. But it wasn't fair—he didn't own all rights to stinging comments.

'You haven't been around enough to know anything about selection,' Jud came back.

'I've been around enough to know who I enjoy being kissed by,' Lucy returned.

'And you think you wouldn't enjoy being kissed by me?'

Lucy gave him a single look, 'Huh!' she scoffed. 'There's kissing and kissing. I've been kissed by you before, remember—your kisses leave me cold.' She hadn't meant to sound challenging, but too late realised that was how he would construe her words.

'Do they now?'

Lucy didn't know when to leave well alone. 'I'd get as much enjoyment out of kissing a—a piece of hard rock,' she said, and was rather pleased with that metaphor.

'You know, Lucy,' Jud said slowly, almost conversationally, 'you really can't expect me to leave this room with that remark unquestioned.'

Lucy looked at him, her head coming up quickly, and too late saw what she had done. Once more she had challenged him—challenged him when she had been warned not to do so again. She wanted to say, I'm sorry, I take it all back, but there was no time, for suddenly there was no longer two feet of carpet dividing them. Jud was close up to her, yanking the protective shield of her linen top out of her hands, tossing it down on the end of the bed and saying coolly, 'We don't want to crush it, do we, Lucy, not if you intend to wear it for the journey home.' Then for the smallest part of a second he looked into her face, saw the staggering astonishment there that the lace front of her petticoat was now against the warmth of his shirt-fronted chest, then his head was blotting out the light, and inside moments Lucy was experiencing at first hand that being kissed by Jud in no way resembled her mouth coming into contact with consolidated minerals.

Oh, she resisted, fought against him, but he was holding her hands behind her back, his own hands not touching her body, but her body felt alive nonetheless as she felt his heat, felt his chest move as her firm breasts were pressed into him.

She tried to keep her mouth tightly closed, and when Jud lifted his head and asked softly, 'Still rock?' she bit back, 'Yes,' refusing to respond, for all the oddest of sensations were passing through her body. That 'Yes' was all the time she had, for again Jud's mouth closed over hers and finding her lips were still firmly closed his mouth moved from hers to trail kisses down the side of her throat and back again to kiss first one corner of her mouth and then the other, and Lucy had to hang on grimly to the thought, I don't want him to kiss me, I don't. But when she was foolish enough to open her mouth to let a husky, 'Don't,' escape, Jud was quick to seize advantage of her parted lips and claimed possession with a lightning speed that shook her almost as much as the knowledge that she didn't want to say 'Don't' any longer.

Without her knowing it, the stiffness left her body and she became a yielding, pliant woman in his arms, so that when his hands let go the hold they had on her wrists, instead of beating and clawing at him as she knew she must, her hands got no further than to come up to rest on his shoulders.

Then all the kisses she had received in the past, and if she was honest she had not allowed too many, were as nothing, and she knew she had never been so shockingly, mind-bendingly kissed before. Jud's hands were making a nonsense of her spinal column, and when he eased her down on to the bed she was only half conscious that the part of her that should be saying no was being swamped by the part of her that wanted to say yes, yes, yes.

'Still rock?' Jud's voice came from above her head, and she opened her eyes to find he was staring down at her a

look of warmth, a look of desire in his eyes for her. Word-
lessly she looked back at him, and he said softly, 'Don't
fight it, Lucy.' Then his mouth was over hers again and her
lips parted and she was responding, was putting her arms
around him to pull him even closer. When his hand came
to push the lacy straps away from her shoulder, she made
no objection. She felt his lips on the swell of her breast
and gloried in the feel of that mouth she had once thought
so hard that was now warm, sensuous and exciting as he
aroused her further.

But when his hand came to cup her breast, it was pure
instinct that had her own hand moving his away, instinct
making the last-ditch gesture to stop this before it was too
late. Jud's body stilled in what she knew afterwards to be
a listening stillness, and she was half relieved, half sorry
when he made no further move to press home his advantage, but took his hands away from her altogether.

Opening her eyes, Lucy saw he was looking down into
her face and she looked away, the intimacy between them
making her shy. Then Jud was putting her straps back into
place, then pulling her into a sitting position and reaching
for her jacket that was all anyhow at the foot of the bed.

'Put your jacket on,' he instructed her quietly, and while
Lucy automatically obeyed, too bemused to do anything
else—he must have known her resistance was only shyness,
only token—yet he had let her off when she had known he
had wanted her as she wanted him.

Jud got off the bed as a small sound on the top of the
stairs reached Lucy's ears, and hurriedly now she buttoned
up her jacket, and was standing too when Mrs Hemming
paused at the open doorway on the way to her own room.
Lucy saw Mrs Hemming glance at the rumpled cover on
the bed.

'Jud?' Mrs Hemming said, and there was a question in
her voice.

'It's all right,' said Jud, going over to her. 'No harm has

come to Lucy—I just couldn't resist coming in and taking up the advantages of being an engaged man.'

Lucy looked from one to the other; she knew her face was scarlet telling its own tale. Mrs Hemming was giving her a look in return as if asking if she could believe her son.

'We ... we didn't get too carried away,' she said, her voice sounding most peculiar in her own ears. She had no idea how it must sound to the two people watching her.

'I'm sure you didn't,' Mrs Hemming said at last, and Lucy knew she believed her. Then in an old-fashioned way Mrs Hemming added, 'I'm sure Jud has too much respect for you for that.'

Respect! Lucy thought when they had both gone. She had acted little short of wanton. She had been beginning to believe from Jud's remark that morning that he no longer thought of her as a hardened female, that he had been beginning to respect her a little, but by her very action of yielding to him, clinging to him, she had shown she was very little different from any other female of his acquaintance, and she knew that apart from his mother and Lottie, and possibly Vera Stanfield and her daughter, he had minuscule respect for any of the female race.

Mrs Hemming's manner was perfectly normal with her when Lucy descended the stairs after fifteen minutes spent in her room trying to pull herself together and pluck up courage to face Mrs Hemming and Jud. He was in the room too, but if Mrs Hemming thought she and Jud were the most unromantic couple she had ever known from the way they acted in public, for the life of her Lucy could not acknowledge his presence.

'All set to go?' he asked.

If he hoped he would force her to look at him then he was in for a disappointment, Lucy thought as she fixed her eyes on a point over his shoulder so Mrs Hemming would think she was looking at him. 'I've left my case in the hall.'

'Jud was just saying he would come up and collect it

when you walked through the door,' Mrs Hemming inserted, and Lucy couldn't have been more relieved that she had beaten him to it. She felt she had nothing she wanted to say to him, but judged that alone once more in her room with her, Jud would lose no time in taunting her with her passionate response to him. As it was, the drive home had to be got through—there would be no Mrs Hemming seated in the back seat this time to make things easy for her.

Since Jud had already said goodbye to Lottie, Lucy went to see her while he took her case out to the car, and when she joined him and his mother on the drive outside, Mrs Hemming turned to her and hugged her warmly causing the sting of tears to hit Lucy's eyes.

'I hope this has been the first of many visits, Lucy,' Mrs Hemming told her sincerely. 'There will always be a welcome here for you, both before and after your marriage.'

What she said in reply Lucy couldn't clearly remember, but she was glad Jud didn't say anything for quite some time once they were on their way; she felt too choked up for one thing, Mrs Hemming's obvious sincerity weighing heavily on her. She knew if Jud said just one word while she was despising herself so much for her part in deceiving his mother, she would instantly have flared up and she and Jud would be at each other's throats.

As Jud drove on, chosing a route that took in more of the English countryside in high summer, Lucy's spirits began to get on a more even keel. Her eyes caught the glint of emeralds and diamonds on her finger and she faced the fact squarely that if she had been prepared to give up her most cherished possession, this weekend at Malvern need never have happened. The choice had been hers, and since she had elected to go through with it, all the blame, she reasoned, couldn't be placed at Jud's door—though she would never forgive him for the way he had kissed her; that he had been unforgivable. She wasn't ready yet to face the thought that Jud had had very little trouble in getting her to respond to him.

'Still hating me like hell?' Jud's voice dropped into the silence she had thought was going to last the rest of the way to Priors Channing. He had given her plenty of time to get her feelings under control, she realised, but she wasn't ready yet to enter a debate on what her feelings for him were—she would probably only earn some more of his stinging sarcasm anyway, she mused, if she gave an affirmative answer to his question.

'Isn't the countryside beautiful at this time of year?' she said tritely, looking out of the window. 'I never knew there were so many shades of green.'

She thought at the very least Jud would have something to say about her ignoring his question, but no, it seemed he was perfectly prepared to go along with her, and answered in kind without any hint of sarcasm in his voice. And suddenly, when she had thought she never wanted to speak to him again, there was an easy flow of conversation going backwards and forwards between them, and after another half an hour had gone by, Lucy forgot her animosity so far as to be ready to talk of her brother whose name she had just mentioned in relation to a meeting of the Young Farmers' Club she had attended with Rupert.

'What work does your brother do?' Jud enquired, his voice showing polite interest.

Lucy wondered if anyone of the people Jud had met since moving into the Hall had conveyed to him that Rupert had never worked at a paid job in his life.

'Er—actually, he's only just finished his education,' she told him, loyalty to her brother making her ready to defend Rupert to the very end if Jud thought it about time Rupert showed some intention of getting his hands dirty.

'What's he been studying?' Jud asked quietly, none of the aggression she had been ready for evident.

'Farm and estate management,' Lucy supplied, then be-

cause she couldn't say with any truth anything about jobs
Rupert had applied for, she added, 'He's studied awfully
hard to learn as much as he could.' That was certainly true.
Poor Rupert—she wondered if he would be in when Jud
dropped her off at Brook House.

Silence reigned between her and Jud after that, but it
was not an uncomfortable silence, and they were nearly at
Priors Channing before Jud suddenly asked:

'Feeling better?'

'Better?' she queried.

'You were near to tears when you said goodbye to my
mother, weren't you?'

She had been, but hadn't thought he had noticed—he
was more observant than she had thought. 'I suppose I was
overcome by guilt,' she confessed at last. 'Especially when
your mother said there would always be a welcome for me
at her home.' She looked across at Jud and saw him nod, as
if to say he knew how she felt, while keeping his eyes on
the road in front.

'If it's any consolation,' he said, 'when my mother saw
your face, flushed from responding to being made love to,
it fully convinced her that everything is as it should be between us—she now has no further anxieties about us.'

It was little consolation to Lucy, though she took small
comfort that for the moment at any rate, Jud's mother
would not be concerned about them, but her face flamed
anew at Jud's bald statement of fact that she had responded
to him. She wanted to deny it, but knew any denial would
be futile—Jud couldn't help but be aware of how she had
reacted to him.

'You knew your mother was coming upstairs, didn't
you?' she asked croakily instead.

'I heard a movement at the bottom of the stairs,' Jud admitted.

Lucy went hot and cold at thoughts of the scene Mrs
Hemming would have witnessed had Jud's hearing not been

so acute—she knew the sound she herself had heard would not have penetrated had Jud still been kissing her. But now he was clearly telling her that her charms were not sufficient to make him lose his head completely. He hadn't been so far gone that his hearing was deaf to all sound the way hers had been.

'That's why you stopped making—kissing me, wasn't it? My showing you I didn't w—want to go any further had nothing to do with it.'

'That's why I stopped making love to you, Lucy,' Jud said, having no trouble in calling what they had been doing by its proper name.

'Would you have stopped if you hadn't heard your mother on the stairs? Would you have ignored what I wanted?' It seemed important to her to establish that she had been the one to call a halt.

'I stopped making love to you, Lucy, out of respect for my mother,' Jud said coolly. 'We were in her house after all, and the slow rate she's forced to climb the stairs is a fair indication of her heart condition.'

Lucy had nothing to say to that. She took in what he was saying about his mother's heart trouble—by calling a halt to the passion that had raged between them he had saved Mrs Hemming from seeing something that would have given her a shock she could well do without—but the thing that stuck, stuck and hurt, was what he had said about his respect for his mother, underlining yet again that he had little or no respect for Lucy Carey.

'In that case,' she said stiffly, her delicate chin held firm because suddenly she was feeling decidedly weepy, 'it's just as well I got tired of your experiment and had physically said no to you anyway.'

It appeared Jud was in no mood to argue further with her. He neither agreed nor disagreed with her, and as Lucy stole a look at him, she could see from his remote expression that he was now feeling as fed up about the whole episode as she was. He wasn't going to rise again to any taunt she could make—he had given her jibe about getting tired of his experiment, scant interest, and that if anything made Lucy feel worse; she felt her remark had been cheap and unworthy of her and knew she had only made it as a face-saver.

The rest of the way to Brook House was completed without another word being said. Lucy didn't care if she never spoke to Jud again and was sure he felt the same way about her.

She saw Rupert's car parked in front of the house, but even the joy she should have felt at seeing it and knowing that at least Rupert wasn't out somewhere with Archie Proctor was missing.

'Rupert's home,' she said more for something to say than anything else as she got out of the car and waited for Jud to extract her case. She wondered if she should ask Jud in and introduce him to her brother, but didn't want to. And then Jud was handing her case over to her, saying without words that he had no intention of entering Brook House.

'Thank you for . . .' she began in a stiff little voice.

'Thank me for nothing,' Jud interrupted her harshly, and she was left staring after him as he got into the high-powered Bentley and went without a single glance at her.

Lucy entered through the front door having half expected Rupert to have seen Jud's car and come out to greet them, but there was no sound of movement anywhere in the house. Thinking that alternatively Rupert must have seen them and had nipped into the kitchen to put the kettle on ready to greet her with a cup of tea—he had always been thoughtful in the old days—she dropped her case in the hall and went along to the kitchen, but there was no sign of him there. Strongly suspecting now that he had had a heavy night and was most likely in bed catching up on his sleep, Lucy went back along the hall and pushed open the sitting room door, to find Rupert sitting slumped down in a chair, his face paler than ever she had seen it.

'Rupert!' she exclaimed, shaking off her own depression at the sight of him. 'What ever's the matter? You look dreadful—are you ill? Shall I . . .?'

'I'm perfectly well,' Rupert assured her, flicking her a brief look and away again, the light tones she was used to hearing from him sounding dull and dejected.

'Well, you certainly don't look it,' Lucy said candidly, trying not to let him hear her concern for him in her voice now that her initial shock was over.

'I've told you, Lucy, I'm perfectly well—don't fuss,' he said snappishly.

Lucy bit down a snappy retort of her own, facing squarely that she hadn't been in the brightest of moods herself when she'd come in, but the last thing she wanted to do was to nag Rupert into feeling more unhappy than he looked.

He was refusing to look at her, and her mind took off in all directions wondering what had gone wrong to make him look so dejected. His car had been standing on the drive, so he hadn't had an accident with it, thank God.

'I'll go and make a cup of tea,' she said, wishing she could do something more practical to help him, but until he chose to tell her what was troubling him, she would have to bottle down the half dozen wild ideas that darted in from all corners. 'Have you had anything to eat today?' she asked when her offer of tea brought forth no response.

'Haven't felt like anything,' Rupert said sullenly, and that in itself told her something was very wrong, for miss breakfast he frequently did, but he had always had something inside him by two o'clock even if it was only a ploughman's lunch at the pub.

'Something is wrong, Rupe—I know it is,' Lucy insisted, determined to get to the bottom of it.

'For God's sake stop fussing!' Rupert flared back

nastily, and Lucy's cheeks went ashen that the brother she loved so dearly could use such a tone to her. He relented at once when he saw her stricken face. 'I'm sorry—I didn't mean to snap. Go and make a cup of tea, there's a pal.'

Rupert came into the kitchen while she was fixing him a bacon sandwich and waiting for the tea to brew. 'Sorry about that,' he apologised again, and seemed to be making a determined effort to cheer up. 'I do have a bit of a problem,' he confessed, 'but ...' as Lucy looked at him, her eagerness to help whatever it was evident in her face, 'but I'd rather handle it on my own—all right?'

Looking at him Lucy thought he still looked dreadful, but at least there were signs about him now of the brother she knew and not the snarling person he had been in the sitting room. It came to her then that at twenty-five Rupert was keen to assert his manhood, came to her that it offended his male pride to have his younger sister wanting to take his problems as hers.

'All right,' she agreed quietly, while still admitting to pangs of sisterly concern, then brightly, 'Now come and eat this bacon sandwich, you'll handle whatever it is better with something inside your stomach.'

Rupert made an effort to appear normal once he was sitting at the kitchen table with his tea and sandwich before him. 'How did your weekend go?' he asked.

Since it was obvious that he had problems enough without hearing how little Jud Hemming respected her—not that she would have told him how Jud had kissed her in any case, she was determined to forget that as quickly as she could—but with Rupert still looking pale, Lucy made out that she'd had a fabulous time.

'And is Jud Hemming still the cold brute you thought he was?' Rupert asked.

Colour surged through Lucy's face at her brother's question—so much for forgetting about Jud's experienced kisses, she thought, as she waited for her colour to subside before she answered her brother.

'Ha, ha,' jeered Rupert with a brother's lack of inhibitions and showing signs of coming to life. 'That blush tells its own tale.'

'I . . . It wasn't . . .' Lucy had no idea what she wanted to say, but seeing Rupert had drawn his own conclusions and in doing so was looking remarkably more cheerful, she thought to bear his teasing if in doing so it cheered him up. 'Jud Hemming isn't so bad when you get to know him,' she mumbled, and went on hurriedly to describe the beautiful views that could be seen from Malvern. Then when she thought she had talked enough about the weekend to give her brother the impression that she wasn't hating her engagement as much as she had previously given him to believe, she asked, 'Are you going out tonight?' adding quickly, thinking he might be feeling a little sensitive about any questions she asked him, 'I'm not prying, only if you're staying in I shall have to see about getting a meal.'

'I'm not going out tonight,' Rupert told her, and Lucy couldn't help but be glad that for one night at least she didn't have to wonder what he was getting up to with Archie Proctor leading the way.

Rupert was up shortly after her the next morning. Lucy had set her mind to be cheerful even though she had slept only fitfully, her mind taken over by unwanted thoughts of Jud Hemming being thoroughly fed up with her—and thoughts of how that didn't bother her in the slightest—chased by worried thoughts of what it was that was worrying her brother. One look at his face told her that if she had slept only fitfully, then Rupert had slept not at all.

It was difficult to bite down her concerned enquiry and try to remember that Rupert was set on being his own man, but she just managed it, saying lightly, 'The paper's come —you can read it while I cook you some bacon and eggs.'

'Not for me, thanks.' Rupert buried his face behind the paper Lucy had dropped on the kitchen table.

Again Lucy stifled the urge to remind him that he had only picked at the meal she had prepared for him last night, and busied herself tidying up the kitchen. At nine o'clock Rupert put down the paper and stood up, looking all set to go out.

'Early date?' Lucy tried to joke.

'Seeing Arbuthnot at ten.'

That was the second time in a very short while Rupert had been to see the bank manager, and Lucy's spirits hit the floor as it came to her that one of the problems uppermost in Rupert's mind was a money problem.

'You'll be taking your bed there next,' she said, still trying to keep a surface lightness between them. Rupert went out without even answering.

CHAPTER SEVEN

IT was impossible to get Rupert off her mind as she waited for his return. His face had seemed haunted somehow when he had left the house—he hadn't purposely refrained from giving her so much as a 'Cheerio' when he had gone, of that Lucy was convinced, it was just that his mind was so full of other things he had been only half aware that she was there.

All thoughts of Jud Hemming and the way he had no respect for her ceased to occupy her mind as she worried over her brother. She was definite in her belief that his problems were financial, she was aware he had an overdraft but had no idea how much, and she wished with all her heart that their solicitor, Mr Gittings, would release some of the inheritance Rupert was due to come into when he was thirty. Mr Gittings had been adamant when they had both gone to see him shortly after their parents' death, and though sorry about the pressing financial straits they found themselves in, he insisted there was nothing that could be done to break the will.

'I have consulted one or two specialists in this field,' he had told them, letting them know he had done everything in his power to help them, 'but your grandfather was a very shrewd gentleman and there's not a loophole anywhere that will allow so much as one penny to be released until the legatee attains the age of thirty.'

Lucy barely remembered her grandfather, but remembered her father referring to him as a 'wily old goat' who having made his money the hard way had told her father he wasn't going to have it frittered away by any young jackanapes who hadn't learned a thing or two. Grandfather's belief that it was impossible to have learned a thing or two until one was thirty was no help to them now, Lucy thought sadly as she waited for Rupert's return.

During his absence she set about cleaning some of the upstairs rooms. Her own room was already tidy, but the bathroom needed attention and she knew without looking that Rupert's room would look as though a hurricane had hit it, but she was glad to be busy and hoped that by keeping herself occupied she would stop herself from looking at the clock every five minutes.

She was still upstairs when she saw Rupert's car pull on to the drive, and without waiting for him to get out of the car she dropped what she was doing and raced downstairs. Half way to the front door she stopped as it came to her if Mr Arbuthnot had not been able to give Rupert any help, then her brother was hardly likely to appreciate her bounding out to ask what had happened.

'I'm in the kitchen,' she called, when she heard the front door open and close. 'Want some coffee?' She heard Rupert's tread coming along the hall and found her hands shaking as she placed cups and saucers on a tray. All of a sudden she was afraid to turn round—afraid to read what the expression on Rupert's face would tell her.

Rupert's voice asking, 'Have we any Scotch?' had her whipping round, and one look at his face was enough to tell her he didn't want the Scotch as a celebratory drink, but to help him over the shock he had received.

'We haven't any,' she began, remembering that he had finished off the remains one day last week, then unable to bear looking at his haggard young face any longer without knowing what caused him to look so beaten, she said gently, 'Do tell me what's gone wrong, Rupe.'

Rupert dragged out a chair from beneath the table and Lucy waited in an agony of suspense while he sank heavily down on to it, then without looking at her, he said brokenly, 'Gone wrong? About everything, I should say,' and went on to further enlighten her, telling her that on top of the seven thousand pounds he already owed the bank, he had tried every way he knew to pay off the debt, but had only succeeded in being in debt for a grand total of seventeen thousand pounds. The coffee forgotten, Lucy pulled out a chair from beneath the table and sank down on to it in much the same way as Rupert had done.

She hoped against hope she had misheard him, but knew with dreadful certainty she hadn't, and wanted to fire questions at him in rapid succession as her mind boggled under the weight of the amount of the debt. She hadn't known it was anywhere near seven thousand, and that in itself was earth-shaking enough, but *seventeen thousand* ...

'We owe the bank seventeen thousand pounds?' she asked when she thought her voice would come out without sounding shrill and frightened, but needing to make sure she had heard right the first time.

'Not all of it's owing to the bank—Arbuthnot is asking for the recall of the money he loaned me to clear Father's debts,' he told her miserably. 'The other ten thousand I owe to Archie Proctor.'

Still trying to recover from the news that Rupert had kept the full extent of their father's debts from her, Lucy whispered, 'Archie Proctor?' and felt her blood turn to ice. She knew this was not the time to rant and rave at Rupert about his friendship with the man whose very name sent a shudder along her spine, but she knew with the sureness that night followed day what had happened, and couldn't help the one word that fell harshly from her lips. 'Gambling,' she said, and when Rupert didn't answer her voice grew accusing. It had been her father's predilection for that questionable sport that had got them into this mess in the first place. 'You've been gambling,' she accused.

'Yes, I have.' There was no heat in Rupert's tones, he just sounded thoroughly crushed as he asked, 'What would you have done, Lucy? I was desperate. At one stage I owed

Arbuthnot ten thousand and he started belly-aching for his money—I managed to reduce the loan to seven, but he was soon on at me again, saying since there was nothing going into the account something would have to be done. He cheered up when I told him you were engaged to Jud Hemming.' Lucy closed her eyes at that, then opened them to force herself to think only of the point at issue. They would get nowhere if she stopped to consider how Jud Hemming would feel at being used to stave off their creditor.

'But now he's dunning you for the money?' she asked. She would get round to Archie Proctor in a minute, for the present she was trying to take in everything in logical sequence. She had been engaged to Jud for less than a week; she would have thought since Rupert had said the bank manager had cheered up on being acquainted with that news, his good cheer would have lasted longer than a week. 'What happened to make Mr Arbuthnot so eager for his money suddenly?'

What Rupert had to tell her did nothing to ease the panic growing within her. Apparently Rupert in company with Archie Proctor had gone to Tambridge, the other side of Dinton, where Rupert had been seen losing heavily at one of the clubs there, by none other than Charles Arbuthnot's son Justin. What Justin Arbuthnot had been doing in such a place was not clear, because according to Rupert, it was well known locally that Justin was more pious than pi. Rupert had started out on a winning streak and had thought to make enough to clear the bank and have some over, but his luck had turned and he had finally come to his senses to realise he wasn't going to win and that not only had he lost the money he had won at the races that day, but since Archie Proctor had been urging him on, lending him more and more money to play with—he had reeled away from the tables in a daze and had bumped smack into Justin, who had been merely watching. When Justin had sat down with him, Rupert, still in a state of shock as it began to sink in that he owed Archie Proctor ten thousand pounds, had been too shaken to keep the information to himself and had revealed to Justin exactly how much he owed Archie.

'So you think Justin told his father?' Lucy asked, having some idea how Rupert must have felt because she was feeling decidedly shaken herself.

'Of course he did,' Rupert said sharply, beginning to show signs of irritation at his sister's question. 'I'll bet the little sneak couldn't wait to get home to tell his father.' Lucy didn't see it quite like that. It would have been the natural thing to do, she thought, seeing that Justin's father must have stuck his neck out to lend Rupert money in the first place, but she thought better than to say so, as Rupert was saying aggressively, 'Old Arbuthnot was on the phone to me before he could have had his breakfast on Sunday morning saying he wanted to see me.'

'And he told you today he won't wait for his money any longer?' Lucy asked, not seeing how Mr Arbuthnot could say anything else since he was aware that her brother had blown ten thousand at the gaming tables in one night. She desperately wanted to cry but held back the tears. Rupert was feeling sick enough as it was, he would clam right up if she allowed her tears to fall, and if there was a way out of this mess—and heaven knew she couldn't think of one—it would need her and Rupert to work it out together.

'He wants his money without delay,' Rupert confirmed, 'as does my *friend* Archie. God, you were right about him, Lucy.' Lucy kept quiet—it was far too late for 'I told you so', even if she could be that cruel. 'I'd hardly put the phone down after Arbuthnot's call when Archie Proctor rang asking—no, demanding,' Rupert amended, 'he rang demanding his money. Oh hell, I wish I were dead!'

'*Rupert!*' Lucy was out of her chair without being aware that she had moved and gone to put her arms around him. 'Don't say that, love—don't say that.'

'Sorry,' Rupert came round out of his self-pity aware

that his sister had her arms around him. 'I didn't mean it—I'm much too curious about life to want to be out of it. Be a love and make me some coffee.'

He stood up to go out when their coffee was finished, and Lucy was relieved when he said he wasn't taking the car. She wouldn't have any peace until he came back had he intended taking his car, knowing his mind wouldn't be on his driving and anything could happen. 'Going for a walk,' he told her as he left. 'I've got some thinking to do.'

Lucy had some thinking of her own to do when he had gone. It was no good thinking 'poor Rupert' over and over again, that wasn't in any way constructive to getting them out of this mess, but where they were going to find seventeen thousand pounds from she couldn't begin to think. She was partly to blame, she could see that now; she should have enquired more closely into their finances. She had known things weren't too rosy and she had been a drain on Rupert too for all her appetite was small and looking after the big house had been a full-time job, but she resolved, regardless of what Rupert said, that as soon as she had had a talk with him she was going to see about getting herself some paid employment.

Rupert had been gone about an hour when the answer to their money problems came to her. Her brother had refused to sell Brook House before and move into something smaller, but he must see now that it was the only way out. Would Rupert agree though? Lucy tried to think of another way, but there was no other way. No, if Rupert would agree to sell Brook House, and she didn't minimise the wrench that would be for him to sell it, but if she could get him to agree then they should have enough money after repaying the seventeen thousand to buy a smaller house, and if they both found jobs all their worries would be over.

Feeling in a much lighter frame of mind and ready to answer every one of the 'againsts' Rupert would have to combat her plan, she kept herself busy while looking out of the window every now and then for a sight of her brother returning.

Rupert, she saw when he at last arrived home, seemed much better for his walk, and she wondered if he too had come up with the same answer as she had. But when she outlined her thoughts, Rupert it appeared had not been thinking along those lines at all, and refused point blank to even discuss the possibility of selling Brook House.

'I know how much you love the house,' Lucy pleaded when she saw all her entreaties for him to sell were being tossed aside, 'but we have to get the money from somewhere and unless you can come up with a better idea we shall be pitched out into the street anyway.'

'Ah, but I do have a better idea.'

Lucy looked across at him, eager to know what he had come up with that she had missed. Then her eagerness fled as the one idea she dreaded flitted through her mind. 'You're not going to try gambling again? Oh, Rupert, please ...'

'I've finished with gambling,' Rupert told her stonily, letting her know he had learned his lesson the hard way. Then warmly he went on to tell her his idea, and Lucy listened speechless, her eyes growing wide, until he came to the end of what he obviously thought was a brilliant idea, and looked across at her to see what she thought.

When she found her voice she left him in no doubt what she thought about his brainwave. 'No,' she said bluntly, and in case that hadn't sunk in. 'Quite definitely no, Rupert —I don't know how you could suggest such a thing! To expect me to go to the Hall and calmly ask Jud Hemming for seventeen thousand pounds—no, Rupert,' she finished firmly, 'I will not do it.'

Rupert seemed entirely insensitive to what he was asking her to do; she could see he saw nothing wrong in what he proposed, and he argued his point for a good five minutes till in the end she felt almost like screaming at him.

'No, no, no, Rupert,' she said again. 'It's out of the question. Jud Hemming and I aren't that close, for one thing.' She knew from her brother's disbelieving expression that he was remembering the way she had blushed yesterday. 'And for another he already has a bee in his bonnet about gold-digging females—I have no wish to be placed in the same bracket.' She had thought that after Rupert's bombshell this morning she no longer had any pride about people locally knowing their circumstances, but she had been secretly hoping they could pack up and leave Brook House without Jud knowing either—she had thought it would take the rest of her engagement period for everything to be completed. 'Besides which,' she added on, looking away from her brother, 'besides which, I don't want Jud Hemming to know how desperately hard up we are.

'He knows already,' Rupert scoffed.

'He doesn't,' Lucy contradicted. 'He knows we no longer employ staff, but he's not aware how bad the situation is ...'

'He's nobody's fool, though, is he?' Rupert inserted sulkily. 'When I saw him ...' He stopped as if he was aware he had made a slip, the look on his face guilty, Lucy thought.

'You saw him?' she asked quietly, then suspicion sped in, though she wasn't sure what she had to be suspicious about. 'You've met him, haven't you?' she asked, and was certain as she said it that he had.

'I didn't mean you to know,' Rupert answered, refusing to meet her eyes, and a feeling of foreboding took hold of Lucy as his statement sank in that somehow, somewhere, the two had met, but for some reason Rupert hadn't wanted her to know about it. She couldn't understand why Rupert, or Jud for that matter, should keep quiet about knowing each other, could think of no reason why she should be kept in the dark about it.

'Why the secrecy?' She was trying hard to keep calm,

but was experiencing a feeling that told her she hadn't heard everything Rupert had been up to yet. 'Why, Rupert?' she repeated, and Rupert looking at her saw a look of determination about her that had him seeing her as an adult woman for the first time, a woman with a right to be consulted on any matter that concerned her. 'I insist on knowing why it is I shouldn't know you and Jud Hemming have already met,' she went on when he still hadn't answered her, refusing to look away from him, and after some moments of hesitating, Rupert dropped his eyes.

'If you must know,' he said, his own aggression rearing its head, 'I never did lose your ring—I sold it to Jud Hemming for three thousand pounds.'

It didn't sink in straight away what he was saying and for a full five seconds Lucy stared at him in stunned disbelief, then as the full force of what her brother had said hit her, she could only disclaim, 'No, Rupe—you couldn't have done. You're joking—you lost my ring when you took it to be polished and cleaned—you told me you had.'

'I know what I told you,' Rupert replied, his conscience pricking him at his sister's disbelieving expression, 'but I was lying. Oh, I took your ring to be polished and cleaned all right *and* asked for it to be valued so that it could be insured, then I forgot all about it until the jewellers rang up and said it was ready. By that time we knew there wasn't any money in the kitty, but I went to collect it anyway and when they said how much it was worth I nearly dropped. Then this sales bloke said any time I wanted to sell it they could always find a buyer, and the idea struck me that three thousand would keep Arbuthnot quiet for a while.

'But it was my ring,' Lucy whispered, her mind trying to take in what Rupert was saying while thinking that he was the person who had sold Jud Hemming her ring. Rupert was the person whose name Jud had known all along—Jud had even got proof of that because he had told her he had a bill of sale, but he had refused to tell her who ...

'I know it's your ring,' Rupert said edgily, 'but you didn't care about my feelings when you wanted me to sell the house, did you?'

Lucy held her tongue. It didn't seem to have dawned on her brother that what he had done was as good as stealing, and she thought better than to tell him she would never have sold the house without his knowledge even if she had been able to do so.

'So, without thinking about how I would feel, you sold Mother's ring,' she said quietly.

'Oh, don't make a fuss about it—I needed the money and there was this chap in the jewellers saying he'd have no trouble finding a buyer, and when I asked who would want to buy a ring with such an old-fashioned setting, he told me that only that morning the new owner of the Hall had been in and enquired about such a piece ...'

'So you went to the Hall, showed Jud the ring and he bought it?'

'That's about the size of it,' Rupert was saying when Lucy stood up and moved to the door. 'Where are you going?' he asked, taken by surprise at her sudden move.

'Up to the Hall,' Lucy said flatly.

'To ask Jud for the seventeen thousand?' Rupert asked hopefully.

'Like hell,' Lucy retorted inelegantly.

She went straight to her room where she took the emerald and diamond ring off her finger and looked lovingly at it for the last time. Then reaching for the box it had come in, she placed the ring inside its velvet bed. Now was too late for tears—she had told Rupert she was going to the Hall, and she had every intention of doing just that; she felt sickened to the very heart of her that her brother could do what he had done. How could he have sold something which belonged to her and which he knew she held so dear?

Looking at her watch she saw there would be little point in going to the Hall for an hour or so. Jud, she imagined, would not be there, would probably be at his place of work. She hoped he was not out of the country, for everything that was honest within her told her she wouldn't rest until she had delivered the ring back into his hands—to leave it in the charge of his housekeeper until he came home wouldn't do.

She slumped down on her bed, her mind shooting off in all directions. Why hadn't Jud told her he had bought the ring from Rupert? It was for sure he knew Rupert was dishonest—she'd told him herself the tale Rupert had told her about having lost the ring. Strangely it wasn't the fact that Jud knew of Rupert's dishonesty that upset her—she had always been loyal to Rupert and would much prefer that Jud didn't know, of course, but it sickened her to her heart that Rupert could have done such a thing, so much so that she began to wonder if she could stay living in the same house with him any longer. Oh, she still loved him—nothing would break the bond that had grown between them over the years, but having discovered a new side to her brother, while appreciating the worry that had necessitated his action, she found she could not accept it.

For the next hour and a half Lucy stayed in her room, then when she thought she had given Jud enough time to have arrived home, she washed and changed into a light-weight button-through dress of pale lemon and applied a touch of make-up to her eyes and mouth. She was going to go to see Jud, hand over the property she no longer had any right to, and after that she would return to Brook House. It was in her mind to telephone her aunt in Garbury to see if she could go there for a few days. She felt she just had to get away and she had always got on well with her mother's sister. Yes, she decided, she would go away to Aunt Dorothy's; perhaps after a few days away from Priors Channing she might not feel so sick at what Rupert had done ... She popped the small square box in her handbag, not looking at the ring again. Then with stiff resolution she went out to her car, not saying goodbye to Rupert who as far as she knew was still in the sitting room where she had left him; his car was still on the drive at any rate.

It wasn't that she was feeling antagonistic towards her brother—it was too late for that too—it was just that she hadn't spoken another word since she had left him earlier, and she had an idea that to get into conversation with him now would have the tears of hurt pouring down her face. When she saw Jud Hemming she had to be as cool and unemotional as she knew he would be—perhaps later in the privacy of her room she would be able to relieve her feelings.

Mrs Weston, Jud's housekeeper, opened the door to her. They had met on the evening she had dined with Jud and his mother. Mrs Weston was a short, stocky woman whom Lucy had liked, and she opened the door wider when she saw Lucy there. 'Mr Hemming is in his study,' she said, smiling.

Mrs Weston obviously thought that as she was Jud's fiancée, Jud would have no objection to her going straight in to see him, but Lucy wasn't so sure—if he was in the middle of something it didn't augur well for this interview she was beginning to get cold feet about, for all she had every intention of going through with it. But the last thing she wanted was for the interview to start off with him snapping at her for interrupting him.

'I'll wait in the drawing room,' she told the housekeeper, then forcing a smile, 'Perhaps you will tell Mr Hemming I'm in there.'

She should have telephoned first, Lucy thought, as she paced about the drawing room. It had crossed her mind to do that, only she hadn't wanted Jud to begin asking questions over the telephone.

She had her back to the drawing room door when it opened, and she swung round as it closed to, half expecting it to be Mrs Weston coming to tell her she had told Jud she was here. But it wasn't Mrs Weston who looked at her across the plush carpeting, but Jud himself, looking stern and remote in the dark material of his business suit. Lucy remembered the last time she had seen him, remembered all too well that he had no respect for her and felt more sick than ever as she battled to keep the tears at bay. If he said, this is an unexpected pleasure, in that sarcastic way of his, Lucy knew she would just fling his ring at him and run. But he didn't say anything of the sort, and his voice when it came held not the slightest hint of sarcasm.

'You look serious, Lucy,' he said quietly, leaving his position by the door and coming closer to look down into her pale face. 'What's wrong?'

'I ... I ...' His gentle tone was affecting the tight hold she was exerting on her feelings. She wanted to tell him, indeed he had a right to know, but just then she didn't trust her voice not to let her down. Dumbly, she undid the clasp of her bag, withdrew the square box and handed it to him.

Jud reached for the box she was offering and at the same time caught hold of her ringless left hand. Then still holding her hand he transferred his gaze to her face, then softly asked, 'Why?'

Just that and no more. If she had thought anything about his reaction at all, it was to think he would be mildly furious that she had thwarted his plans to keep Carol Stanfield from mooning over him, but his quietly asked 'Why?' had her wondering what exactly he was feeling—those cold grey-green eyes were telling her precisely nothing. Wrenching her hand away from his, she looked down at the small expanse of carpet between them, inconsequently noting that his shoes looked expensive and hand-made as he stood so near to her.

'Why, Lucy?' Jud asked again when her answer was a long time in coming.

'I know—I know who sold you the ring, Jud,' she said at last, unable to look at him with the shared knowledge that her brother was little better than a thief between them. 'It m-makes our bargain null and void . . .'

'Why does it?' Jud asked. 'You were fully prepared to go through with it when you didn't know from whom I purchased the ring.' His tone was still quiet, reasoning even.

But Lucy didn't want to be reasoned with. Jud was so clever he could make black seem white, and white appear to be black, and as far as she could see there was nothing to be reasoned with. Jud had paid for the ring—it belonged to him . . .

'It's different now, Jud,' she said slowly. 'You paid a lot of money for the ring, and . . . what's mine is Rupert's, so there-therefore I sold it to you and . . . and I have no right to it . . .'

'So you want to back out of our bargain?'

She wasn't sure there wasn't the faintest suggestion of an edge creeping into Jud's voice, but she still couldn't look at him—she didn't want to see the scorn in his eyes, to see the contempt there. She knew he was thinking she was as dishonest as her brother by breaking her word to be engaged to him for three months.

'No, I'm not backing out of our agreement. If you still want Carol to think we're engaged, that's all right with me, but I can't wear your ring, Jud.' Silence followed her words and she wished she could look at him to show him she was sincere, but she was afraid to read what might be in his expression when he looked back at her.

She gave a startled movement when one of Jud's hands came to rest gently on her shoulder, the other coming beneath her chin to lift her face up so he could see into her eyes. 'If you can't wear it, Lucy, won't you take it and keep it for the three months we agreed?'

She looked at him then and saw none of the harshness in his look she had expected to see, but an understanding she had never thought he would have for her. Oh God, she couldn't help thinking, I'm going to howl my eyes out if I don't get out of here soon.

'I ... I can't take it, Jud,' she said huskily. 'It ... It wouldn't be right.'

'It belonged to your mother,' Jud reminded her, which was the last thing she needed to be reminded about at that moment. 'I know how much the ring means to you.'

For all Jud's hold on her was gentle, Lucy had a distinct feeling his grip would tighten if she followed her instinct and made to run from the room. Gallantly she stayed where she was to reiterate in a voice that was now decidedly wobbly, 'I can't take it—what's the point anyway?' and as the first tear fell and others fell in quick succession she struggled on, her face wet with tears, 'It will be just as hard to part with it in August as now.'

She felt Jud's hand on her shoulder move in a convulsive movement, and as she looked at him saw his face unlike the face she knew, and realised he couldn't bear to see a woman in tears. And when she knew she should stop crying if only to take that look away from his face, she realised something else, that instead of his look drying her tears it had more tears raining down her face. I love him, she thought, and couldn't think how it had happened, and dipped her head so that he shouldn't see or hear if a groan of the despair she was feeling escaped her.

'Don't cry, Lucy,' Jud said raggedly. 'If the ring means so much to you, then keep it—it's yours with no strings attached.'

'Oh, Jud!' Lucy groaned, and lifted her head to gaze in wonder that the man she loved was nowhere near as cold and as hard as she had believed him to be. Then, sanity trying to assert itself, she wiped her face with the back of her hand, her tears still falling, and told him haltingly, 'I can't take it—wh-when I've gone, you'll think my tears were j-just gold-digging tactics—and ...'

'Gold-digging tactics—you?' retorted Jud, taking his handkerchief from his pocket and gently smoothing away her tears. 'You wouldn't know where to begin,' and while Lucy could only stand and stare at him, he pulled her closely into his arms and tenderly kissed her.

Quite when things began to get out of hand she wasn't sure, but suddenly the tenderness of Jud's kiss gave way to a stronger emotion and his mouth was gently seeking and parting her lips with his own while his strong arms held her firmly to him, leaving her with no clear idea of anything any more other than that this was where she wanted to be. Then as Jud broke the kiss and loosened his hold slightly to look down at her, she masked her gaze as the thought came crashing in from nowhere that she would only have to look at him for him to know the depths of her feeling for him—he had no respect for her now. To have him know she loved him would be the end.

It wasn't easy to stiffen her body and drag herself out of his arms—she never afterwards knew from where she got the will-power to do it—but Jud made it easier by not insisting that she stay where she was, and Lucy, knowing where all other pride had deserted her, that it would soon be all over the village that she and Rupert were hugely in debt, the pride of unreturned love gave her the strength to whip up a note of anger in her voice, when in truth she wanted to yield and melt against him.

'You said there would be no strings attached,' she reminded him, glad to hear her voice sounding coldly angry. 'What was that kiss supposed to indicate—an avowal of your honourable intent?' She saw Jud's lips firm in a hard line, and didn't at all like the look on his face now, but forced herself to go on. 'Well, let me tell you, Jud Hemming,' she said, while the inside of her was breaking up, 'let me tell you I don't want any favours from you that you'll want payment for later—If you think . . .'

She got no further, for with an angry oath Jud made no apology for, she felt herself hauled up in his arms with savage anger as he turned with her and almost threw her down on to one of the deep and wide settees the drawing room held. Then before she had regained her winded breath, she found Jud's body lying over hers, and he was kissing her with a fierce fury such as she had never known.

There was no tenderness in his kisses now, just the torrid heat of anger that was spurring him on as he claimed her mouth again and again. Uncaring of any protest, she managed to gasp when his mouth left hers to plunder kisses from her throat and chest, Jud let his anger take him on a pillaging sortie that had her dress unbuttoned, her shoulders bare and her breasts revealed to his darkened, furious view.

'Let me up!' Lucy screamed, her face scarlet as she tried to cover herself from his livid gaze, while knowing she had brought this on herself for spurning what she rightly knew to be his offer of giving her her ring without any thought of payment in cash or in kind.

Her protests were useless as Jud bent his head to devour the nectar from her breasts, his strong hands behind her hips pressing her body into him, making her aware for the first time of a man's body when passion had him aroused.

Almost fainting with fear, she felt her lips claimed yet again and knew an awakening feeling within her that had no right to be there, because this wasn't the way she wanted him to love her. When his hands left her hips to hold in his warm palms the throbbing swell of her breasts, though still pressed hard beneath him, she took advantage that at least his hands were no longer anchoring her down, and moved her body as though to get nearer to him, though secretly thinking that would be an impossibility, and when Jud

stilled for a moment as if undecided what her movement
indicated, she gave a superhuman push, found herself free,
and dived for the door, grabbing her bag as she flew. It
didn't matter to her then what she looked like with her
dress undone from top to hem, her lacy lingerie all anyhow; all that mattered was that she was away from him.

But when Jud sat back on the settee, his legs crossed in
an indolent position telling her he had no intention of coming after her, she made a fumbling attempt to do up one or
two buttons while still watching him carefully.

'Like I—said, Jud,' she said, nothing about her cool now
as her words came out in gasping breaths, 'you can keep
your favours.' And with that she turned blindly, yanked
the door open, and raced to her car.

CHAPTER EIGHT

Lucy never expected to sleep that night. Her emotions were frayed ragged—thoughts about her brother's problems, the new side to him she had discovered were enough to keep her awake without the never-to-be-forgotten scene up at the Hall. She remembered hoping before that she would never be around when Jud let go his temper, how right she had been to be wary, she could have done without being on the receiving end of it.

Hot colour surged through her cheeks as she lay in her bed willing sleep to come. She couldn't help but wonder if Jud's fury would have taken him on to what had seemed likely at the time. Supposing she hadn't been able to escape? Would Jud have let his passionate anger take him on to possess her?

More tears came as she relived the scene. Thank God Rupert had been nowhere about when she had arrived home. It was the first time in an age she had been glad he was out—who he was with was of no concern to her as she had drawn her Mini up outside Brook House and let herself in. She had been shaken by the sight that had met her eyes in the hall mirror—her dress decidedly the worse for wear, the wide-eyed, tear-ravaged face so sad and unlike her own, she had hurried past the mirror and had gone straight to her room.

She lay awake for what seemed like hours, but eventually sheer exhaustion sent her into a troubled sleep, and she awakened to find Rupert beside her a cup of tea in his hand.

'This is the second time I've been up,' Rupert effected a

grumbling tone. 'I thought you were never going to wake up.'

'What time is it?'

'You've been crying,' Rupert countered in return. 'Your eyelids are all swollen,' and then turning away believing he was the sole cause of his sister's tears, he sank down on the pink velvet-covered sewing chair. 'I'm sorry, Lucy,' he muttered, his voice sounding so miserable, so low and dejected, Lucy wanted to go and put her arms around him and tell him everything was all right—but everything was nowhere near to being all right. 'God, I'm sorry.'

'My tears weren't all on account of you.' Lucy couldn't help trying to ease his burden.

'Jud Hemming give you a bad time?' Rupert was shrewder than she had given him credit for, Lucy realised, as her brother swivelled round to look at her.

'He was very kind, actually.' Well, he had offered to *give* her the ring, hadn't he? Her mind refused to try and cope with what had happened afterwards. Then she explained the rest of her tears to Rupert, 'I came home feeling a bit sorry for myself after I'd handed the ring over.'

'I've never known you feel sorry for yourself in my life,' Rupert said stoutly, while seeming to accept without a second's thought that Lucy had parted with her ring.

'There's always a first time—now I'd better get up.' Rupert stood up to go, but Lucy called him back. 'I thought I'd go and stay with Aunt Dorothy for a few days, Rupe— I ...'

'Wish I could come with you,' Rupert said as he left her room. Lucy knew he meant he wished it was as easy for him to escape from his problems—he couldn't know, because no one was going to know her secret, but she wouldn't be leaving the problem of loving Jud Hemming behind. She thought it would follow her wherever she went, and for evermore.

When Lucy got up and washed, she saw the tell-tale

signs of her weeping reflected in the bathroom mirror, and
bathed her eyes in cold water to find that that didn't do
very much good. Ah well, she shrugged resignedly, she
wasn't going anywhere today, and since her friends had
stopped calling since she had refused invitation after invitation, there was little chance of anyone seeing her except
Rupert.

When she rang her aunt an hour later, her aunt was delighted to have her to stay. 'I haven't seen you since the
funeral,' she said gently. 'When are you coming?'

Lucy thought for a second or two; she would like to give
the house a thorough clean before she went. 'Would Friday be all right?'

Going in search of Rupert after she had put the phone
down, she found him staring moodily out of the sitting
room window. 'I've just rung Aunt Dorothy,' she told him.
'She sends her love—I'm going on Friday.'

Rupert accepted this piece of information without comment and continued to stare out of the window. Lucy
wanted to ask him what he had been thinking about when
she had come into the room, but realised her question was
unnecessary; Rupert's thoughts were despairingly trans-
parent.

Then suddenly Rupert dropped his moody air. 'I'm going out,' he said, his face showing sudden resolve, and before Lucy could ask where he was going, he supplied, 'I'm
going to see Archie Proctor to see if he'll wait for his
money.'

Lucy watched his car roar away down the drive, knowing he had grown fed up with the inactivity of staring into
space with his thoughts going over and over the same old
problem. She couldn't see that going to see Archie Proctor
would do very much good, instinct telling her Archie was
much too sharp to let her brother promise to pay him at a
later date when there was no likelihood of Rupert finding
the money from anywhere.

Dressed in shorts and a loose-fitting cotton top, Lucy set about the housework. She would give the downstairs rooms a good clean out today, she thought, and tackle upstairs tomorrow. For what was left of the morning she was busy in the sitting room, vacuuming, polishing, dusting, flinging the windows wide open to let the sun come streaming in. At lunch time she felt hot, dusty and tired, but a ten-minute sit-down with a cup of coffee and a piece of toast removed the tiredness, making her wish she could get rid of thoughts of Jud that perpetually crowded in so quickly. Trying not to think of him was useless, she found, for as soon as she had banished him from her thoughts, fixing her mind on something else, he would again come unbidden to her mind. Trying once more to eject him from her thoughts, she wondered how Rupert was faring— he had been gone a long time; perhaps he was having trouble in finding Archie Proctor.

After rinsing the few things she had used for her light lunch break, Lucy looked round the kitchen and decided that was next on her list. Then having cleaned all the surfaces, she looked at the kitchen floor. More often than not she cleaned it over with the long-handled sponge mop, but today, more from the need to keep herself thoroughly occupied, she filled a bucket with hot soapy water and armed with a scrubbing brush and floor cloth, placed the movable furniture on top of the kitchen table and got down on her knees.

It was a large area to scrub, as she knew from previous experience, and a hot June day was perhaps not the best time to do it, even with the windows open and the back door standing wide there was little breeze to cool her, but she carried on and had almost finished with just one more patch to do, when she thought she heard the sound of a car round the front. Rupert, she thought, and knowing he couldn't have news other than bad, carried on with her scrubbing, thinking to make him a cup of tea when she'd finished.

Her head down with beads of sweat clinging to her fore-head making the hair around cling damply to her brow, Lucy was unaware that anyone had entered the kitchen until two hands came clenching hard at her waist and she was set bodily to her feet. Her *yowk*! of surprise was broken off, colour surging through her cheeks, as gaining her balance she swung round and saw Jud Hemming standing there looking angry enough to hit her, but before she could find her voice and ask him what he thought he was playing at, he was taking in the appearance of her long legs with knees grubby where she had missed the kneeling mat, seeing her eyes still showing evidence of last night's weeping, noticing the sweat of honest toil clinging to her, and was biting into her.

'Surely to God there's no need for you to do that?' he snarled.

Jud knew they were broke, what was the use in pretend-ing? Lucy thought as the pink flush died from her cheeks and she tried not to be alarmed by his very obvious anger. 'Who else would do it?' she snapped back, and as he took a step nearer found she wasn't as brave as she thought she was, and added, hating herself for backing down, 'A-any-way, I've finished the floor now.'

'Then go and get cleaned up,' Jud bit at her. 'You look terrible.'

'Thanks.' She knew she looked terrible without having him confirm it, and pleased to find her anger against him returning. 'I'll go and get cleaned up when I'm ready.'

Jud looked at her steadily and she thought some of his anger was diminishing until he said with a dangerous quiet-ness which told her he wasn't fooling, 'I'll come and put you in the bath myself if you're not out of here in one minute.'

'Damn you!' she exclaimed, knowing it was no idle

threat, but she went just the same, and just to be contrary when she would have loved a bath, she stood under a refreshing lukewarm shower for ten minutes and pondered on the reason for Jud's visit.

She had never thought to see him again—well, apart from perhaps bumping into him in the High Street. Perhaps he had come to apologise for his behaviour last night —no, he wouldn't do that—if she was honest they were both partly to blame; she had goaded him into doing what he had done by throwing his more than generous offer back in his face. She was drying herself off with a towel before donning fresh underwear and a pretty summer dress of lilac-coloured cotton when she wondered if his mother was ill. The thought upset her for a while until she reasoned that Jud wouldn't have come to tell her that anyway, and if his mother was ill he certainly wouldn't come storming to Brook House so violently angry—which gave rise to the thought, had he been angry before he had seen her on her hands and knees scrubbing the kitchen floor? She dismissed the thought; she could work herself to a grease spot and Jud Hemming wouldn't care.

He was still in the kitchen where she had left him when she came down. The room had been put to rights, she noted, as she glanced cautiously at Jud, all the chairs were neatly pushed in against the table and her hastily abandoned bucket had been emptied and was standing on the floor near to the cooker.

'Where's your brother?' he asked without preamble, as she stood uncertainly by the door, his eyes going over her, nothing of whether or not he approved of the change in her appearance showing in his face.

'He's out,' she said shortly.

'In that case I'll talk to you.'

Briefly Lucy wondered if it was Rupert Jud had come to see, and felt angry that he should feel he would make do with her. She wanted to say a sarcastic 'I'm honoured', as she had done once before, but suggested instead that they move to the sitting room, and as Jud followed her in she paused to wonder how she could think of being sarcastic when what she wanted to do was to fall at his feet and beg him to love her the way that she loved him.

Jud waited until she was seated before taking the seat opposite her—she was struck again by his natural good manners and firmed her lips so none of the softness in her was apparent to him.

'What plans have you made for the future?' Jud asked, coming directly to the point. Lucy had known it wasn't his way to shilly-shally around, but the question caught her off guard, and her eyes widened as it came to her that somehow or other Jud knew the extent of the trouble they were in.

'I'm going to stay with an aunt of mine for a few days on Friday,' she said, looking away from him, playing desperately for time—she knew he didn't mean immediate future, her going away for a few days didn't concern him in the slightest, but since Rupert had settled nothing about the money he owed—even if Archie Proctor had agreed to wait, which she doubted—she wasn't about to tell Jud anything.

'Quit stalling,' Jud said sharply, letting her know she could disappear to the moon and never come back and it wouldn't bother him. 'I happen to know your brother is in debt way above his idiotic neck.'

Lucy let his comment about her idiotic brother ride, though she was sorely tempted to flare up at that even though in her own opinion Rupert's gambling had been more than idiotic. 'What makes you think my brother is in debt?' she asked instead with as much civility as she could manage, and thought Jud wasn't going to answer her, then with a look that said, All right, if you want it with no holds barred, here goes, he said:

'I didn't think too much behind the reasons for your brother selling me a piece of jewellery. He had a jeweller's estimate of its value made out in his name, I naturally thought it belonged to him—if I thought about his reason for selling it at all I probably put it down to the fact that it was something he no longer had any use for; he had told me it had belonged to his dead mother. When you came to the Hall claiming the ring as yours I realised your brother had stolen it from you.' Lucy winced at the word 'stolen', and Jud paused briefly before going relentlessly on. 'It was then I knew he must be in very bad straits financially— especially as I could see how much the ring meant to you. Then when I came to see you I noticed there didn't seem to be any hired help about the place.' Lucy saw Jud's glance flick around the room, telling her he knew that as well as the absence of staff, some of the furniture was absent, too.

'Yes—well, perhaps we are a little hard pressed at the moment,' she agreed, though not seeing it as any business of Jud's.

'More than a little hard pressed, I would say,' Jud said coolly. 'I happen to know your brother owes at least seventeen thousand pounds.'

Lucy looked at him aghast. 'H-How do you know that?' she whispered, all pretence gone from her now.

'I made it my business to find out,' Jud answered, and only then did Lucy begin to wonder why he wasn't at his office; he was casually dressed in sports shirt and slacks— surely he hadn't taken the day off to pry into their affairs? 'As the supposed fiancé of Lucy Carey of Brook House, I'm privy to certain information about you,' he added.

'Mr Arbuthnot,' Lucy uttered incredulously. 'The bank manager told you?' She was out of her chair, furious that Charles Arbuthnot had released to Jud, in the guise as her fiancé, confidential matter he had no business disclosing. 'He had no right . . .' she began furiously.

Jud neither confirmed nor denied that his informant had been the bank manager, but ordered her sharply to, 'Sit down—I'm here to try and help.'

'Help?' Lucy queried. Jud Hemming was the last person she wanted help from, but she sank down again as he had ordered.

'Yes, help,' he confirmed. 'Now shut up and just give me the answers I want.' Lucy was too dumb struck on being commanded, and in her own home too, to 'shut up' to do more than look at him. Then while she was searching round for some suitable sarcastic comment to floor him with, he was saying, 'You told me your brother had studied farm and estate management—is that right?'

Not knowing why she was answering him at all, though thinking it might be something to do with Jud's authoritative air that commanded an answer, she found herself saying, 'Yes, that's right. Rupert is fully qualified, he's very good at it, he ...'

'And is he seriously looking for a job?' Jud broke in, and again Lucy found herself answering.

'Yes, he is—but he doesn't want to move away from Priors Channing.'

'Right,' said Jud. 'Jack Gilbert has been helping me out, but he's past retiring age and wants to go as soon as I can find someone qualified to look after the interests of the farms and properties attached to the Hall. Tell your brother to come and see me, and if he's as good as you say he is, I'll take him on a three months' trial.'

'But—but ...' Agitatedly Lucy stood up, her heart brimming over with love for this man. He was trying to help, proving he wasn't as cold as he was looking now, and she dropped her eyes, not wanting him to see the love she had for him shining from her eyes as she struggled to get her words out. 'I know he'll be thrilled at the chance of working in Priors Channing,' she said quietly, while hoping Rupert would take advantage of the wonderful opportunity Jud was offering, but ... The light went out of her eyes; no matter how much money Jud would pay him, Rupert couldn't hope to settle the huge sum he owed.

'You're worrying about the seventeen thousand?' Jud asked, noticing her sudden stillness and coming to stand beside her.

Lucy nodded. 'Rupert comes into some money when he's thirty,' she said, and looking at Jud had a suspicion he knew about that too. 'In five years' time he'll be able to pay the money off, but I can't see anyone waiting that length of time, can you? And Rupe refuses to sell the house—it's all so impossible, isn't it?' she ended flatly.

'Not so impossible,' said Jud, causing Lucy to look at him quickly, hope rising high within her as though expecting him to have thought of something both she and Rupert had overlooked. 'If Rupert works for me, he will obviously need somewhere local to live—there's a house available, but since you say he won't give up Brook House, I'd be prepared to buy this place off him and give him a written undertaking to sell the house back to him when he comes into his inheritance—meantime he can settle his debts and still live here.'

Lucy wanted to sit down at the shock of having all Rupert's worries so easily dealt with. She felt near to tears again, and couldn't help thinking that the man she had fallen in love with was certainly some man.

'Why are you doing all this for Rupert?' she asked, her brimming eyes looking at him, ready to give him anything he asked in return. She saw from the way his eyes frosted over as he looked at her that her gratitude was the last thing he wanted.

'I'm not doing this for your brother,' he stated coldly. 'I'm doing it for you.'

'For me?' Lucy's own expression hardened and she rapidly changed her mind that she would give anything he asked to the man in front of her, who now looked cold and forbidding. Then bluntly, because she wanted a straight answer, one she didn't have to cogitate the meaning to, though wondering if he would lose his temper again if she suggested as she had last night that he wanted payment from her for what he was doing, she asked, 'Why?' and waited for him to tell her.

Jud looked at her, saw from her expression that she had already made up her mind what his reason was, and with that cold hard stare she knew, repeated, 'Why?' Then, his very tone insulting, 'Because my women never go away from me with less than they came—why else?'

For all of two seconds Lucy looked at him, unable to believe what she had heard, then fury that transcended anything she had ever felt before raged through her at his cutting jibe—Jud Hemming was placing her firmly in the same class as his other gold-digging female friends, and without time for thought Lucy rode high on emotions that said her outraged feelings had to be relieved in some physical act. Her hand came up with lightning speed, and the crack of her furious hand echoed round the room as she hit him with all her force across the side of his face. Then the room stilled as Jud went white and a murderous light entered his eyes, and terrified now at what she had done— a dull red mark was already appearing before her eyes on the side of his face—Lucy waited in fear and trembling as Jud moved towards her, waited for him to knock her senseless.

He halted only when he was near enough to read the real fear in her eyes, then told her in a voice that splintered with ice, 'Do that once more, Lucy Carey, and the loss of your precious virginity will be a certainty.'

He meant every word—God, how he meant it—and too frightened to utter the merest syllable in case Jud let go the reedy hold he had on his temper, Lucy stood looking mutely at him, too scared to even say, 'I'm sorry.'

Then Jud, his teeth firmly clenched together, took one deep and audible breath as though still fighting with his self-control, and grated, 'I'll expect your brother at the Hall tonight.'

What Lucy's feelings were when he left she couldn't begin to know save that it penetrated that Jud was a far bigger man than she had even realised, for in receipt of such a vicious blow, and her hand was still stinging from the force of having administered it, he was still prepared to consider employing Rupert.

She was still trembling with fright knowing how close Jud had come to losing the thin thread of control he had over his rage, and fell back in a chair wishing Rupert would hurry up and come home. Jud's visit had left her exhausted; she didn't pretend it was her used up energies in scrubbing the kitchen floor that had left her this way, she was young and tired though she had been from her physical efforts her healthy body was soon revitalised. Jud had asked for that slap, but oh, how she wished she had held it back! She doubted that even if she did bump into him in the High Street now, he would deign to acknowledge her, and she knew that to have him look icily through her as though she didn't exist would be unbearably hard to take.

She was deep in thought, reflecting that she had never been Jud's 'woman' for all he had implied that she had, and longing to have been just that—at least she would have her memories, for she felt sure he would initiate her tenderly and she had seen too little of his more gentle side to store with her memories—when Rupert arrived home.

She hid her despondency as she saw the same misery she had been experiencing showing in Rupert's face. Archie Proctor, she knew without asking, had given her brother the thumbs down.

'He won't wait,' Rupert confirmed, and went on to tell her he had gained a firm suspicion from something Archie Proctor had let slip that if not exactly owning the club he had taken him to that night, then Rupert was sure Archie Proctor had somehow stood to gain by egging him on when he had begun to lose. 'God, I was wrong about him,' Rupert muttered, staring hopelessly into the fireplace. 'He's evil Lucy, evil. When I think of him smiling as he lent me more and more money ...' Lucy could see Rupert was tearing himself to shreds. 'When I think of how green I was ...'

'Forget about it, Rupe,' Lucy said gently, feeling as sick as her brother must have been on finding out that Archie Proctor had set him up. 'Jud ...'

'Forget it?' Rupert looked back at her scandalised. 'How the hell can I forget it?'

'Put it behind you for a minute, then,' she persuaded. 'Jud Hemming has been here and wants to see you.'

'Wants to see me?' Rupert asked, hope breaking out in his face. 'Did you ask him to lend me the money? Did he say he would?—I'll pay him back every penny with interest. I ...'

Lucy could see Rupert was getting excited as the idea took hold and knew she had to stop him straight away. 'I didn't ask Jud to lend you the money,' she said, and saw the light go out from his face. 'But,' she added hastily, 'Jud has a proposition to put to you—he wants you to go up to the Hall tonight.' And when Rupert asked charily what sort of a proposition, Lucy outlined what Jud had told her, and because she thought her brother's initial reaction to selling Brook House to Jud would be a definite no, and knowing Jud wouldn't make his offer twice, she told him about that too so he would have a couple of hours to think about it before turning Jud's offer down.

Rupert heard all she had to say, his open face revealing one expression after another, his voice eager putting in a question here and there, but he didn't ask the one question she had thought he would ask, the same question she herself had asked, 'Why is he prepared to do all this?'

She was rather proud of her brother when he came to see her before going up to the Hall in the early evening. In general Rupert was uncaring about the way he looked. He never looked scruffy and his clothes were not cheap, but as she looked at him as he came into the room, she saw he had

donned his best suit and brushed his fair hair into some
sort of order, and was looking very much the part of someone who took seriously his forthcoming interview.

'Will I do?' he asked.

'You look fine,' Lucy said, and added softly, 'Good luck,'
and went out with him to his car to watch him drive off.

She had over two hours to wait for his return, he was
being much longer than she had anticipated, and she tried
unsuccessfully to settle down to some embroidery as the
minutes ticked by, but gave it up as a bad job as in her
mind's eye she pictured the two men she loved most in the
world, the one with a love that forgave him the idiocy of
his latest stupidity, the other that would forgive him whatever he did.

She wanted to fly to the door when she heard Rupert's
car pull on to the drive, but forced herself to sit where she
was. She would know from Rupert's face as soon as he came
in whether things had gone well or not. She heard his key
in the front door and composed her features not to look
anxious. Then he was in the room with her, his face
solemn, his eyes after one hurried look in her direction
looking away from her, and despite her resolve not to be
upset if his interview had gone badly, the words escaped
her:

'Oh, Rupe, I'm so sorry ...'

But before she could say more, Rupert was lifting his
eyes, the light in them refusing to be hidden as a beaming
smile threatened to split his face in two.

'You wretch!' she beamed back. 'You got the job.' Then
she was out of her chair and mindless that they had never
been a demonstrative family, they were hugging each other,
and Rupert was laughing as they both settled into chairs
and he leaned forward to tell her:

'He's a great man, Lucy.' That much she knew, and she
listened to Rupert telling her everything that went on.
'Mind you, he didn't give me an easy time, though he did

seem to understand my feelings at finding out that Dad had
gambled away my inheritance, for all he called me a young
ass for attempting to do the same with the rest of it.' She
hadn't thought Rupert would reveal to anyone how their
father had gambled away a fortune, and it showed her how
implicitly Rupert must trust Jud to have done so. 'Jud then
asked if I was completely cured of the urge to gamble and
I told him I'd learned a bitter lesson and nothing would get
me on that tack again.' Lucy felt like crying so great was
her relief at hearing her brother's statement, but she swallowed down her tears and listened intently to what else
Rupert had to tell her. 'We were in Jud's study—he had
maps laid out showing the farms and properties so I would
know exactly what I would be taking on and we went into
every detail of the job first. Then he asked me point blank
"Can you do it?" and looked me hard in the eye at the
same time—— By God, he's a strong character, and it was
funny, Lucy, but his whole attitude seemed to stiffen my
backbone, and I couldn't help thinking, Yes, I could do the
job, or I would die in the attempt.'

Lucy thought she knew what he meant. Jud would demand the best, and he was putting Rupert on his mettle to
prove that he was the best. She had every faith in Rupert,
the wild streak in him that had reared its head following
his disappointment on their parents' death, seemed to have
burnt itself out. 'So what did you say?' she prompted. 'Did
you tell Jud you could do the job?'

'Yes—I told him if he'd give me half a chance he
wouldn't be disappointed, and he gave me another of those
hard looks, and said, "Right—start tomorrow." '

'Tomorrow?' Lucy gasped. 'But . . .'

'That's what I thought. If anything I would have thought
he'd say start on Monday or even the first of the month,
but no, I'm to start tomorrow—Probably doesn't intend to
give me the chance to get into any more mischief,' Rupert
added, but he didn't seem to be offended if that was the

reasoning behind Jud's thinking.

'And—and what about the house?' Lucy asked tentatively.

'We agreed on that too,' Rupert said to her further relief. 'If my trial period is satisfactory—and I'll make damn sure it is—then after that time I'm to arrange to have the house valued and Jud will have his own survey done, then we're to see solicitors and have a legal contract drawn up whereby Jud purchases the house and agrees to sell it back to me in five years' time.'

Everything, it seemed, had gone swimmingly, and Lucy's heart was bursting with happiness for her brother and with undying gratitude to Jud who in spite of what he must think of her had not let those feelings get in the way when helping her brother. Though she still had one worry on her mind and hesitated to take the excited look off Rupert's face. But if she had been watching the expressions that passed over her brother's face, he in turn had been noticing hers.

'You're worrying about Archie Proctor, not to mention old Arbuthnot not waiting three months for their money?' he asked.

'Well, I did wonder,' Lucy understated, not wanting to underline it too heavily.

'That was the only bad moment of the entire interview,' Rupert told her. 'With Jud being so open with me—even if it was a no-holds-barred sort of openness at the beginning—I felt it only right to be honest with him in turn, and I confessed that you'd refused when I'd asked you to ask him for the money—I half wished I hadn't afterwards,' he said, and the bright look left his face momentarily as if he was recalling the way Jud had been. 'He came down on me like a ton of bricks and really sorted me out—the outcome of which being that I now know I'm to stand on my own two feet, and now that I shall be earning, and being paid well, I might add, it was Jud's opinion that we should be able to afford someone to do the heavy work in the house.'

Lucy was still gasping at this as Rupert went on. 'When Jud had finished wiping the floor with me, he went on to suggest he would lend me the seventeen thousand now, to be returned when the house sale is completed, on condition that I was prepared to sign a paper stating that if it could be proved that I had so much as had a flutter on the horses within the next three months, then the seventeen thousand would act as his deposit on Brook House and I would lose all rights to buying it back when I come into Grandfather's money.'

So Jud wasn't taking Rupert's word that he had finished with gambling, Lucy surmised, but any disquiet she might have felt at that vanished under the knowledge that Jud's goodness stretched so far as to advance Rupert the money he so desperately needed. Nor was Rupert offended, she saw when she glanced at him; the look on his face told her he hadn't taken exception to Jud wanting to make sure he was over his wild streak, and the more she thought about it, the more she could see the sense of it. Rupert had said he would never gamble again, and knowing how much her brother thought of Brook House, Jud had ensured that for three months at least Rupert wouldn't gamble. By the end of that time, Rupert should be so far along the path it had originally been intended he would take, even though he would not be working for himself but for someone else, he would be doing the job he had always wanted to do and still be doing it from Priors Channing.

'Well,' said Rupert, getting to his feet, 'if I'm to start work in the morning I'd better get off to bed—it wouldn't do to be late on my first day.'

Lucy went to bed that night with her head full of what Rupert had told her of his interview with Jud. She wondered if she was in for another sleepless night as she lay there with her mind picking up first one part of her conversation with Rupert and then another, to be topped again by feelings of guilt that the man who was doing so much to get her brother out of his plight had that very day been on the receiving end of the furiously delivered blow she had dealt him with her hand. She groaned in anguish and buried her head beneath the bedclothes as though to hide away from all further thoughts of Jud and how she loved him, and surprisingly, she slept.

CHAPTER NINE

RUPERT came home after his first day's work tired, but on top of the world. 'It was marvellous putting some of the stuff I studied into practice,' he told Lucy enthusiastically, and went on to tell her that although he thought he still had a lot to learn, finding actually doing the job varied greatly in parts from the theory, there was no way he was going to fall down on the job. Lucy listened to all Rupert had to tell her with interest while hoping he would mention Jud's name. It was ridiculous, she owned, this wanting to hear Jud's name, wanting to hear what Jud had been doing that day too. But as Rupert went on she learned that Jud had stayed only long enough to introduce Rupert to Mr Gilbert who was looking forward to handing over the reins.

Rupert's conversation over their meal was still enthusiastic about his job, and he went on to tell her how he and Mr Gilbert had spent the day. 'We were in the office most of the time,' he said. 'Mr Gilbert certainly knows a thing or two—I shall have him with me for a week and I intend to learn everything from him I can.' He pushed his dessert plate away from him. 'Lord, I'm tired—I think I'll have an early night.'

Lucy had been half wondering and dreading if Rupert would be going out that night—even if it was only down to the local for a celebratory pint she knew she would have been on pins until he came home wondering if he had fallen in again with any of the set that had led him astray, and on hearing Rupert state he had no intention of doing anything other than going to bed, she realised then that she herself had not been absolutely certain that her brother had given up his old-new ways. She felt guilty at the thought, so much so that undecided through the day whether or not to ring Aunt Dorothy and tell her she wouldn't be coming after all, she now thought to prove her trust in her brother by going, and while she was away, she decided, she wouldn't for one minute wonder if Rupert was getting up to anything.

'Will you be all right if I go to Aunt Dorothy's on Friday?' she asked, and feeling uncomfortable as Rupert looked at her sharply as if guessing her earlier thoughts, 'I meant will you be able to cope—you know, with your meals and things.'

'Of course I can cope—you go. I might give Harry Burnside a ring at the weekend—he'll know if there's any new female blood in the area.'

Lucy laughed at the wicked lecherous look Rupert affected and relaxed. Harry Burnside had been a friend of her brother's in the pre-Archie Proctor days. If he was taking up with Harry and his set again she knew she had nothing to worry over.

On Friday morning after checking that there were enough supplies in the house to keep Rupert going until she got back, Lucy set off in her Mini for Garbury, making good time and pulling in to check the route on her map when she got to Bamford. She had been this way many times, but always before it had been with her father at the wheel and she had been too intent on looking about her to notice much of the route they had taken.

It was raining when she reached Garbury and with the vagaries of an English summer had turned quite cold, but when she drew up outside her aunt's stone cottage, the welcome she received was as warm as was the welcome meal Aunt Dorothy had prepared for her.

Their greeting over, Lucy's case upstairs in the bedroom she was to use, and a meal inside her, her aunt plied her with questions as to how she and Rupert were going on. There had been a few tears shed between them as they had discussed the days when Lucy's parents and Dorothy Varley's sister had been with them, but they both brightened up when Lucy said Rupert was now working, but for all Aunt Dorothy was family and knew of the change in their circumstances, Lucy felt she couldn't tell her any of what Rupert had been up to before he had started his job.

'I'm so glad for Rupert,' Dorothy Varley said sincerely. 'It's what he's always wanted to do, isn't it, and it's good to know the future seems to be panning out.' Then in the way of most female relatives with an unattached niece of Lucy's age, asked, 'And what about you, Lucy? What have you been doing just lately? Any young men on your horizon?'

Painfully Jud sprang instantly to mind. Lucy didn't think Jud could quite be put into the category of 'nice young men'—nice was not the word to describe the man who she felt sure would have raped her had she lifted her hand to him again—but he was the only one she wanted, and in the same way she hadn't been able to tell her aunt about Rupert, she found she couldn't tell her about Jud either, though she wondered if she would have felt better if she could confide in someone about him.

'You're a romantic, Aunt,' she accused softly, and bent to fondle her aunt's all-sorts dog Ragamuffin, commonly known as Muff, who had been allowed in now that their meal was over.

Lucy had always enjoyed her visits to Garbury, and this visit was no exception. Though constantly when by herself or out with Muff whom she took off on long walks, she was always aware that the delights around her as she looked over moors or strolled through woodlands were not as thrilling to her as they once had been, she did find some peace in their splendid solitude.

It was Tuesday of the following week before she thought she ought to give some mind to going back to Priors Channing. If nothing else, Rupert would soon need to have the larder re-stocked, and loath though she was to admit it, she was secretly longing for a sight of Jud. It would be enough just to see him, she thought, and into her mind's eye flashed a picture of him the last time she had seen him. His fury with her then seemed to live and breathe fire on her now as she relived the scene and hurriedly she fixed her mind on anything that would take that image away. That night she broached the subject of going back to her aunt. She had already stayed longer than she had intended.

'I shall be sorry to see you go, Lucy,' her aunt said when Lucy told her she would be going home on Thursday. 'I've so enjoyed having you to stay—you remind me so much of your dear mother—you have the same gentle way with you that she had.' Lucy coloured as she recalled that awful slap she had served Jud with and hoped the need never arose to have to confess it to her aunt. 'I've been meaning to say this the whole time you've been here,' Dorothy Varley went on, not noticing Lucy's heightened colour as she bent to remove Muff's collar. 'But in the event of Rupert marrying before you—and I know you well enough to know you would rather he and his wife had Brook House to themselves—well, I wanted you to know that if Rupert marries first, it would give me the greatest of pleasure for you to come and live here with me.'

'Oh, Aunt,' Lucy said softly. She hadn't given the matter any thought herself, but as her aunt had said, yes, she would want to leave Brook House when Rupert married. There was no 'if' about who married first, she knew without thinking twice that there was only one man she would ever want to marry, and since she might as well cry for the stars as hope Jud would ever want to marry her, she knew she would never marry.

'The house will be yours one day anyway,' Aunt Dorothy went on briskly, seeing a sudden glint of tears in her niece's eyes, which was brought on as much by her aunt's kindness as by her own private thoughts. 'What you do with it when I'm gone won't worry me—I just wanted you to know there'll always be a home here for you.'

Lucy said goodbye to her aunt on Thursday with mixed feelings. She had found a degree of peace in the tranquility that had surrounded her aunt's cottage—though cottage was a misnomer, since it had four bedrooms, each of them being occupied when they had visited as a family, with herself sharing a room with her aunt when Rupert had come with them. She knew, even before her first sight of Jud again, that in going back to Priors Channing any peace she had found would be shattered, for she would be unsettled knowing he was but a few miles away.

Rupert was glad to see her. He had taken Jud's remarks about having someone in to do the heavy work to heart, she discovered, and in her absence had found a Mrs Turton from the village who starting last Monday was willing to come in twice a week to help with the housework. Lucy was pleased to see none of Rupert's enthusiasm for his job had lessened.

'It's great,' he told her after asking after Aunt Dorothy, and making the polite enquiry whether Lucy had a nice time. She could see he could barely wait to get these politenesses out of the way before he told her all he had been doing. But for all he went on to say he was now working on his own, Mr Gilbert having left, Jud's name was barely mentioned save that Rupert had sometimes passed him driving in the opposite direction as they both went to their places of employment.

As the weeks went by Lucy saw nothing of Jud. Not that she expected to; it was hardly likely, she thought, that he would call at Brook House anyway. If he wanted to see Rupert about anything, then he would ask him to come up to the Hall to see him, and even if she and Jud were still engaged, there would be no need at all for him to come and see her since Carol Stanfield and Jud's mother lived many miles away from Priors Channing, and they wouldn't know if he called or not. Briefly Lucy wondered if Jud had told his mother their engagement was at an end and hoped that if he had he had broken it to her gently, though she chased herself round in circles when she reasoned that if Mrs Hemming knew, then Carol Stanfield would know, and that wasn't what Jud wanted, was it?

She gave up worrying about it and went upstairs to change. She intended to go into Dinton shopping soon, and though prior to the shattering discovery that she was in love with Jud it hadn't mattered to her whether she arrived in the centre of Dinton in jeans or whatever she wore, she still had in her mind's eye the picture of bumping into Jud in the High Street.

She had lost weight in the six weeks since she had returned from her stay with her aunt, she discovered when she zipped up the skirt of her lightweight mustard suit. The weather had turned cold again and she rather thought her cotton dresses might not get another airing until next summer, but one never knew. Going over to the mirror to apply a light film of rusty pink lipstick, she noticed hollows in her cheeks that hadn't been there two months ago. She hadn't paid much attention to her face just lately, finding it difficult to meet the pain in her eyes. But now she saw she had a fragile look about her, and not sure she liked it, combed her hair this way and that in an attempt to hide the hollows in her cheeks. It was no good, whichever way she did her hair, she was still left looking the same. In the end, with a thought of, blow it, I'm not likely to see him anyway, she combed her dark cloud of hair into its usual style and went downstairs to grab up a basket on her way out and set off for Dinton.

She needn't have bothered, she thought, a sigh escaping her an hour or so later as she left Dinton behind, her purchases completed. She had seen plenty of other people she knew in the High Street—had avoided by appearing to be in a tearing hurry having to stop and chat to Mrs Arbuthnot, who she felt sure would not have been able to carry on a conversation without mentioning her engagement.

Almost at Brook House she was driving down a narrow lane when she saw a car approaching from the other direction. Colour flared in her face and her stomach churned over as she recognised instantly the sports car that belonged to Jud. She slowed down as she knew she had to when her first impulse was to put her foot down and go roaring past him—if it wasn't for the narrowness of the lane who knows, she thought as the two vehicles crawled towards each other, for Jud had reduced his speed too, she might even have managed a breezy wave as she passed him, but if they didn't want to take the first layers of paint off each other's vehicles and since there was nowhere either end of the lane a car could back into to allow the other to pass, short of reversing the whole length of the lane, they had to crawl by each other.

Her colour subsided when, her window open, she made a play of seeing she did not touch his car, but as they drew level even though she was determined he should think she was concentrating too hard to look at him, of its own will it seemed, her head came up and she looked straight into those cold, hard, so well remembered grey-green eyes, and was struck again as she had been that first time she had spoken to him when she had gone to the Hall to demand the return of her ring, by the remote hardness of the man. She knew then that he had not forgiven her for the swipe she had taken at him.

'Good morning,' she said carefully, her face matching his for coldness, or so she hoped. She felt sick when he refused to answer her and looked away—it was so much what she had feared—then her head was jerking up again to hear him say:

'I've just left Brook House.' She saw his eyes were giving her close scrutiny, but if he noted the hollows in her cheeks, he didn't comment on them. 'I'm having a dinner party at the Hall on Friday night—I want Rupert to be there. I didn't think you would come as his partner unless I asked you personally.'

He was right there. Nothing would get her up to the Hall with or without a personal invitation, much as she yearned for the sight of him.

'I don't know that I shall be free,' she said lightly with the air of someone whose engagement book was full to overflowing, and received one of Jud's icy looks for her trouble.

'Despite all efforts to the contrary,' Jud told her coldly, 'word is circulating that your brother had been ...' he paused, then inserted, 'for the want of a better phrase— letting the side down.' He continued to look at her in that hard way, saw from the way she had grown pale that his words were sinking in, then grated harshly, 'Make sure you *are* free on Friday,' then pressed his foot on the accelerator and moved forward.

Lucy set her own car in motion without realising she had as it came to her with a sinking feeling that gossip in the village, as in any small community, would be rife with the fact that Rupert had been hitting the high spots in company with Archie Proctor. Word was probably out too, no doubt originating from Archie Proctor, that Rupert had been gambling away money he couldn't afford to lose. And while it wouldn't bother Jud one bit what anybody thought of him—the Careys had always had a high standing in the community, and if Rupert was to prove that he was still socially acceptable, then the best way for him to do it was for him to attend Jud's dinner party on Friday night.

But why was it necessary for her to attend as well? The way Jud had issued his invitation had made her think she was the last person he wanted to invite. She was still trembling from her encounter with Jud when she arrived at Brook House and forced herself to drink a steadying cup of tea while she tried to think up every imaginable excuse for not going.

The only trouble was, with half of her wanting to attend the other half of her was sure it was the last thing she wanted, and as one half argued against the other, she could think up no excuse that Jud wouldn't see through, and since he was so determined she should be there she wouldn't put it past him to leave the Hall and come and get her if she didn't show up with Rupert. That very thought made her tremble again, for both their tempers were likely to flare if that happened and she didn't trust herself not to give herself away with some unthinking remark made in the heat of the moment, and Jud was too shrewd not to take apart anything she might let slip—her heart turned over just thinking of Jud finding out that she loved him.

Rupert mentioned the invitation when he came home that night. He seemed unaware that there was any special reason why the Carey brother and sister need attend, but it was obvious that he was quite looking forward to going, and it came to Lucy then that Jud would have had a dinner party anyway—that it hadn't been laid on specially for her brother's sake—she had been so het up after seeing Jud she hadn't been thinking straight, though what Jud had said about Rupert 'letting the side down' and everyone knowing about it did ring true.

When Rupert said, 'You needn't come if you don't want to,' he looked down at her ringless left hand, and for all Lucy hadn't discussed the matter with him, he seemed to be aware that she was still sensitive about it. 'I mean,' Rupert went on, 'if it's going to be an embarrassment to you, I'll tell Jud you're not feeling well or something.' Lucy knew then that she would be going. If any of Jud's guests were ill-mannered enough to look down their noses at her brother, she would be there to give him support.

'I'm looking forward to going, Rupert,' she told him, 'and I won't feel in the slightest embarrassed.'

As she sat before her dressing table mirror putting the finishing touches to her make-up on Friday night, she hoped that lie would see her through the evening; her stomach was already churning over like a cement mixer and she doubted she would be able to eat a thing.

It had been difficult deciding what to wear. She had more than enough dresses in her wardrobe to choose from, but discarded one after the other until in the end she put a stop to her dithering, telling herself it was only dinner up at the Hall for goodness' sake—she'd dined there scores of times before Jud Hemming had bought it, and once since, she recalled, but that didn't make her choice any easier.

When she joined her brother downstairs, she was dressed in a flame-coloured dress of a fine material, that had at one time been a shade too tight, but money being no object in those days she had purchased it just the same, thinking to diet her already slender frame down for a week before she wore it. Tonight it fitted her perfectly, being low at the back, hugging her curves at the front and nipping in to her tiny waist to fit over her hips and fall away in a slight flare at the hem. With it went a matching gauzy stole that did little in the way of keeping her warm, but gave the whole effect a touch of class when draped loosely over her shoulders.

'Wow!' Rupert exclaimed when he saw her, giving her ego the boost it needed. 'I never noticed before, but I've just realised I've got a beautiful sister.'

'You're not so bad yourself,' Lucy replied, hoping he wouldn't perceive how nervous she was about the evening in front of them. 'You should wear a dinner jacket more often.'

Rupert preened himself vainly and made her laugh, then said, 'Well, if the mutual admiration society has finished, let's get going—I'm starving!'

Every light at the Hall seemed to be ablaze as Lucy and Rupert parked behind several other cars on the drive; fortunately Rupert had thought to put up the top of his sports

car so Lucy's hair was not blown about as it would otherwise have been.

On going through the imposing front door of the Hall,
the first person Lucy saw was Jud. He was guiding some
of his guests into one of the main reception rooms, but he
saw her and Rupert and excused himself to come over and
greet them, adding to Lucy, 'You know where the cloak-
rooms are if you want to titivate.' Lucy couldn't get away
fast enough.

She left her brother in conversation with Jud, trying to
control her trembling limbs, she went without apparent
haste to the downstairs cloakroom and stayed there for as
long as she dared. When she came out her brother and Jud
had moved on to where she had seen him shepherding his
other guests, but had stayed in conversation with Rupert
waiting for her. Jud looked superb in his dinner jacket, and
she knew his eyes were on her as she approached.

'Glad you could make it, Lucy,' he said sauvely, making
it sound to Rupert, who was listening, the sort of polite
remark any host would make, but Lucy knew it wasn't, and
it needled her sufficiently to make her lift her head proudly
as a small burst of annoyance gripped her that Jud Hemming thought he had only to snap his fingers and everyone
would come running.

'I wouldn't have missed it,' she replied with quiet polite-
ness, and as grey-green, flint-hard eyes met sparking velvet
brown eyes, she knew they were both aware that a private
battle was going on between them. Then with an easy
charm Jud was escorting them to join his other guests.

'I think you know everyone here,' he said, and Lucy
glanced around the dozen or so people there.

At first they were just a mixed-up jumble of people
dressed up in their best, preparing to enjoy a pleasant social
evening, then when Jud excused himself and went to greet
another couple who had just come in, Lucy saw that indeed
they did know everyone. Charles Arbuthnot and his wife

were there listening to Joyce Appleby holding forth. Joyce, she saw, was accompanied by Gordon Berkeley, so he must be her latest. A waiter hovered with a tray of drinks and Lucy, knowing she would need all her senses about her to get her through tonight, had just smiled a refusal when a gentle voice at her side said, 'Lucy, I'm so glad you could come,' and this time the words weren't said with sarcasm held just at bay, but in a tone that said they were sincerely meant.

Lucy turned her head quickly as she recognised Mrs Hemming's voice. 'Mrs Hemming,' she said, stunned, and couldn't think of another thing to say. She hadn't dreamt Jud's mother would be here tonight. He should have warned her, she thought, an anger against him growing within her. Then the good manners of her upbringing came quickly to her aid and she turned to introduce her brother to Mrs Hemming.

'Rupert and I met earlier today,' Mrs Hemming revealed, causing Lucy to wish Rupert had mentioned it to her, for she certainly wouldn't have attended had she known Jud's mother was here.

She had no idea what Jud had said to his mother about their engagement, but knew she just wasn't up to playing the part of his fiancée tonight—the other people in the room didn't matter—but with the frost between her and Jud only just beneath the surface, Mrs Hemming wasn't going to be fooled by any act she put on. And looking at the warmth in her eyes, so different from the arctic conditions of her son's eyes, Lucy knew she no longer wanted any part in deceiving this woman. Rupert had seen an acquaintance of his who unfairly appeared to have two attractive young ladies to himself, and with a charm that would be quite devastating when he had matured a little, he asked Mrs Hemming if they would mind if he left them.

'He's going to break a few hearts before he's very much older, I'm afraid,' Mrs Hemming opined as they both

watched Rupert make the trio a quartet and saw the smiles
of the two girls turn on to him in the easy acceptance of
their age group. 'Now, my dear,' Mrs Hemming went on,
turning her attention to Lucy, 'Jud has given me strict instructions not to overdo things tonight, for all I'm perfectly well,' she added as a small look of anxiety crossed
Lucy's features. 'But knowing I shall get told off if I don't
obey orders, I wonder if you would come and sit with me
so we can chat?'

Lucy was torn between wanting to stay with Mrs Hemming and wanting to make a bolt for it as panic gripped
her—she knew the subject of her engagement could not
be ignored. Then Mrs Hemming beamed at her with a
mischievous smile that made them conspirators somehow, a
smile that told Lucy Jud's mother wasn't too worried about
the possibility of being told off by her son. Lucy joined
forces and went to sit with her.

She was sitting on a settee beside Mrs Hemming when
Jud came back into the room. He was instantly waylaid by
someone, but she noticed his eyes had gone first to where
she and his mother were sitting before he gave the person
who had buttonholed him his attention.

To her surprise the engagement was not mentioned by
Mrs Hemming, causing Lucy to wonder again what if anything Jud had told his mother. She expected at any minute
that Mrs Hemming would notice her ringless finger and to
comment on it, but she didn't, but carried on talking as
though they were almost mother and daughter, answering
Lucy's enquiry as to Lottie's health without the restraint
Lucy would have thought would have been there if she had
known she was now talking to her son's ex-fiancée.

'Lottie is very well—she asked to be remembered to you
—she quite took to you the weekend you were with us,' Mrs
Hemming told her. Then Jud was standing over them,
saying dinner was ready and assisting his mother off the
settee. Lucy stood up too and for a brief moment her eyes

met his over the top of his mother's head. Lucy felt sick at
the lack of warmth in his look and turned her head away,
her eyes going frantically in search of her brother.

Dinner was not the ordeal she had thought it would be.
The huge table, ornamented as it was with an exquisite
centre floral decoration of small flowers, was round, so
there was no head to the table. But Lucy was startled to
find Jud had placed her to one side of him and his mother
at the other. She tried not to see any significance in this
but knew Jud left little to chance, and felt quite flustered
for a moment until it dawned on her that since no official
announcement of their engagement had been made—or
broken for that matter—while there were other people
present—her eye was caught by Mrs Arbuthnot and they
exchanged pleasant smiles—since her and Rupert's presence here was to show anyone who thought otherwise that
Rupert was socially acceptable it wasn't likely, she reasoned,
that Jud would have Rupert's sister very far away from him,
affianced to him or not.

Her reasoning wasn't very brilliant, but it was the best
she could do, she thought as she struggled to get through
her first course while trying not to be so totally aware of
Jud sitting beside her. She wondered if she was going to
have to sit through the whole meal without addressing one
word to him. Now wasn't the time to apologise for hitting
him, and quite honestly she rather thought she had left it
too late to bring the matter up. But some time during the
evening she ought to be able to bring herself to thank him
for all the help he had been to Rupert—she shuddered to
think what would have become of her brother if Jud hadn't
been there.

'You seem to be struggling.' That was Jud's voice; he
had been talking to someone else but turned to her now,
his voice sounding quiet in her ears amid the buzz of
general conversation. Her eyes flew to his to see what he
meant by that remark—he did have an uncanny knack of

reading her mind. There was a faint smile on his face, she saw—well, he could hardly scowl at her in front of his other guests, could he? she thought, trying not to see anything specially for her in his smile. She saw his eyes drop to her plate. 'No appetite?' he queried in clarification.

'I ... I never was a big eater,' she returned, finding her voice with difficulty.

'We're still on the first course,' he said, reminding her that small appetite or no, she should be making a better job of it than she was doing. Deliberately she placed a forkful of the delicious salmon into her mouth. 'Delightful as you look, Lucy, I shouldn't advise you to lose any more weight.' Her eyes met his—so he thought she looked delightful? His mouth was smiling and at last she observed a slight thawing of the ice in his eyes. 'Perhaps delightful isn't the right word,' he added, and as he watched a faint pink came over her cheeks, purely she realised because she now had his sole attention, and it was so good to see the ice melt. 'I should have said you look stunning.'

'Thank you,' she received his compliment quietly, then was grateful when he turned his head as someone else caught his attention, and as the meal progressed she began to feel better, and won some of Jud's approval by tucking in as more delicious courses followed.

After dinner they returned to the room they had vacated. Lucy found herself with Mr and Mrs Arbuthnot and managed for a few minutes to make surface conversation, but when Mrs Arbuthnot said, 'I was so pleased when I heard about you and Mr Hemming ...' Lucy felt a flutter of panic and couldn't have been more pleased that Joyce Appleby chose that moment to join them, launching straightaway into an item of gossip that had an enthralled Mrs Arbuthnot giving Joyce her full attention, and Lucy, with a silent word of thanks to Joyce, was able to drift away from them.

'Enjoying yourself?' Rupert asked some thirty minutes

later, coming to join her as she entered the room after pop-
ping into the cloakroom to renew her lipstick—she had left
it until now because so many of the other women present
had repaired there after dinner, and she was heedful of the
intimacies that were bandied in an all-women conclave.

'Having a lovely time,' Lucy replied, and as music began
to play and people began dancing she felt a moment's
trepidation as Rupert's eyes went to the blonde Alison he
had been talking to before dinner. Any minute now Rupert
would go and ask Alison to dance, of that she was sure,
which would mean she would be left on her own. Normally
that wouldn't have bothered her, but since Mrs Hemming
had a seat free to one side of her, for all she was in conversation with plump Mrs Sanders who looked to have
taken every diamond she possessed out from under lock
and key for tonight, Lucy felt the pull to go and sit beside
Jud's mother, while at the same time being afraid of what
might ensue from any conversation they had. She owned
she might be being over-sensitive, since she had sat with
Mrs Hemming before dinner and had not been made to feel
uncomfortable in the process, but . . .

'Dance with me, Lucy.'

She hadn't seen Jud coming up to her and reasoned that
he must have just come in through the door behind her.
He wasn't asking her to dance but ordering her to, and she
hated herself for being too weak to refuse him.

Jud's arm came round her as they reached the area that
had been cleared for dancing and although his hold was not
tight, Lucy couldn't have said it was loose either as her
heart began to thump wildly within her. She tried to calm
herself by instilling the thought that she was just the first
of his duty dances.

Jud steered her to the top end of the room, an area that
to give atmosphere was not as well lighted as the rest of the
room, and Lucy thought then what better chance would she

have to apologise than now when he couldn't fully see the expression on her face.

'I'm—I'm sorry I hit you, Jud,' she blurted in a now-or-never plunge. But before she could add more Jud had turned her and they were dancing into the full lighted area —she dared a peep at him to see how he had taken her apology.

Jud was looking down and to anyone watching it would appear he was smiling at her. She waited for his polite comment, for the smile never left his face, and then he said between gritted teeth, 'Shut up, Lucy.'

His reply made her angry, but since he was able to put up a show of smiling, even though that ice was back in his eyes again, she beamed a smile his way and asked, her own eyes cold, 'How can I do anything other when you put it so charmingly?' She had the satisfaction of seeing his smile crack, and then the music came to an end.

Feeling drained from her short contact with him, Lucy felt his arm drop from her and decided to head for the cloakroom until she regained some of her poise, but her intention was forestalled when Jud took hold of her arm— she knew he had felt her tug of protest that would have been missed by anyone else watching, but he ignored it— and led her over to the vacant seat beside his mother.

'Lucy doesn't feel like dancing any more,' he said smoothly, and like it or not Lucy was forced to sit down. She refused to look at him, and after seeing his mother had everything she wanted, he asked Lucy if she would like something to drink.

'No, thank you, Jud,' she answered with a sweetness he would know was assumed if no one else did. 'Dancing with you has made me lightheaded enough without the added stimulant of alcohol.'

She thought Jud was going to laugh, which wasn't what she wanted because he knew as well as she did that her veiled sarcasm was meant to be cutting. She was still

undecided whether or not she had amused him when he
turned to the woman on the other side of his mother and
asked her to dance.

'Not as bad as you thought it was going to be?' Mrs
Hemming queried as soon as Jud and his partner were
away, and Lucy wasn't sure whether Mrs Hemming was
referring to her dance with Jud or if she somehow knew
that she hadn't wanted to come here tonight. 'I didn't mean
to pry,' Mrs Hemming continued when she could see from
Lucy's face that the girl wasn't sure how to answer her. 'I
just thought you might have mixed feelings since you and
Jud have temporarily split up.'

'Temporarily split up?' Lucy echoed, trying to wake up
her brain to do some quick thinking but finding it was still
on its starting blocks.

'I'm not trying to interfere—believe me I'm not,' Mrs
Hemming said gently. 'But when Jud explained that he
thought he had rushed you too much, got you to agree to
marry him when you were still emotionally all at sea after
losing your parents, I couldn't help wondering if there was
anything I could do. Would it help if you got away for a
while? You're more than welcome to come back to Malvern with me if you need somewhere quiet to think things
out.'

'Oh no, thank you, Mrs Hemming.' Lucy's refusal was
automatic, a smile accompanying her words.

'All right, my dear—I do hope, though, that for both
your sakes you'll have something to say to Jud soon.'

Oh, she'd have something to say to him, Lucy thought,
realising now Jud had put the blame on to her for their
broken engagement—well, it had been her who had called
an end to the farce, she recalled in fairness—but for Jud to
have told his mother the break was only temporary, as
though once she had sorted herself out they would be
engaged again, infuriated her. Infuriated her even more
because Jud had put her in the position of not being able

to deny it if she didn't want to upset his mother—he knew how she regarded his mother; he knew she would avoid upsetting her at all costs.

She looked at the people dancing nearest to them, saw Jud was among one of the couples and as his glance looked their way she sent him a smile of pure vitriol when he looked at her and was pleased to see he almost, but not quite, missed his step.

Then someone came and took the seat next to Mrs Hemming and engaged her in conversation, and Lucy was relieved when the conversation extended to her that there was no room in it for talk of a personal nature.

She was glad to be able to catch Rupert's eye when she judged it was time to leave. Jud had not asked her to dance again, she hadn't expected him to—he had read her acid smile all right.

'Ready to go?' Rupert asked, coming over to her. From his face she could tell he had thoroughly enjoyed his evening.

'Do you mind?'

'Not a bit,' he declared, then with a wickedness that was part of the old Rupert, 'Wouldn't do to let the ladies have too much of me on one night.' He grinned down at his sister and she had to smile back at his sauce. 'I'll just tell Jud we're leaving ...'

While Rupert went to see Jud, Lucy said goodbye to Mrs Hemming and those nearby her. Others were still dancing so she knew it would be a general wave as they made their exit, but she felt a tinge of disquiet when Jud joined her and Rupert at the door and showed every intention of going to the outer door with them. If she wasn't still feeling angry with Jud for what he had told his mother, she would have told him not to leave his guests, that she and Rupert could find their own way out, but she didn't trust herself to speak to him without flaring up, and guessed that he knew it too, so she declined to say anything as he

walked with them, mentally preparing herself to offer him
a cool handshake and mouth the usual polite utterances.

At the door, however, her plans to give him a chilly
goodnight were thwarted by Jud addressing Rupert, saying, 'The night has turned cold, Rupert—I imagine with
all the cars here yours is some way away from the door. You
didn't bring a wrap, did you?' he turned to ask Lucy when
she knew very well he'd seen them arrive that he was aware
she hadn't. 'Perhaps you would bring your car up to the
door to save Lucy catching a chill.'

Rupert went cheerfully to do his bidding, and as the
door closed after him, keeping the night air out, Lucy
thought she didn't care very much to being treated like
Jud's delicate great-aunt. He was only doing it to needle
her, of that she was sure. He knew it wouldn't take very
much to get her to lose her temper and challenge him with
what he must know his mother had told her. Deliberately
turning her back on anything that would aggravate her
further, she said the opposite of what she knew he was
expecting.

'I haven't thanked you yet for all you've done for
Rupert.' She regretted that her words came out coolly, and
not in any way as she would have wished them said, for she
was sincerely grateful.

'There's no need for your thanks,' said Jud. 'Particularly
as it hurts you so much to voice them.'

'I'm sorry.' Instantly she apologised, knowing that by
voicing her thanks in the offhand way she had, she had
offended his sense of niceness. 'I really am grateful, Jud,'
she said, capitulating fully, all anger with him forgotten.
'It was very good of you, especially since ...' she stopped
there, realising that in an endeavour to impress on him how
sincere she was she was in danger of saying too much.

'Especially since—what?' he asked, and she knew she
wasn't going to get away without answering him—she
should have known he was too smart for her.

'Well,' she went on, then not liking having to wriggle in front of him, 'well, you said when I asked that you were doing it for me—and I can't think why other than you feel you might owe me something since I couldn't accept your gift of my mother's ring—I . . . and I—meant it was especially good of you since you have no respect for me.'

'Good God!' Jud ejaculated as if it was the last thing he expected to hear. 'What the hell makes you think I don't respect you?'

Lucy was as shocked by Jud's reaction to her statement as he seemed to be on hearing her voice it.

'When . . . when you—kissed me that time—at your mother's house,' she said in a bewildered voice. 'You know . . .' It was stamped in irremovable ink on her mind, he couldn't possibly have forgotten. 'I knew then that you'd lost all respect for me.' The words were dragged from her and she felt near to tears.

'You think I don't respect you because you were human enough to respond to a biological urge,' Jud said as if this was the first time he had given the matter any thought. Then stingingly, as though he in turn was affronted that for all this time she had nurtured the belief that he didn't respect her, 'For God's sake, Lucy,' he snapped, and his voice was now fairly burning into her, 'if I didn't have any respect for you, do you think you would be *virgo intacta* still?'

Her face aflame, Lucy didn't wait to hear any more, but raced to the door and was through it, uncaring if she caught double pneumonia if Rupert hadn't arrived to take her home.

CHAPTER TEN

LUCY was beset by a feeling of sadness the next day, though she did all she could to show Rupert a cheerful face hoping that by the next day she would feel brighter. But when the feeling continued not only the day after but all through the following week, she knew she would have to do something about it. She was well aware of the cause—didn't all her thoughts circulate around Jud these days? She half wished she had never met him, that he had never come to live in Priors Channing, though she felt a confused rush of denial come to oust that wish.

It was ten days now since they had dined at the Hall, and she knew suddenly that it was no longer possible for her to live so near and yet so far away from Jud. Why, she had even begun to give herself excuses why she shouldn't go out, all, she knew, because she dreaded meeting him accidentally, dreaded seeing again that cold look in his eyes that said he felt nothing for her.

She had been happy during the time she had spent with Aunt Dorothy she recalled—well, if not exactly happy, she had been able to find a modicum of peace. While she stayed in Priors Channing every time she did venture out she risked seeing Jud and renewing her heartache. No, she'd had enough. Her mind was suddenly made up. She would get in touch with Aunt Dorothy and take her up on her offer to have her to live with her, and once she had closed the door on Priors Channing, she would see about getting a job. She'd heard it said there was nothing like hard work for getting over unrequited love, but didn't believe it—she had polished everything in sight this morning, and Jud had been with her with every movement.

Lucy decided to tell Rupert her decision as soon as he came in, but the light in his eyes, the excitement that was all around him as he breezed in through the door put what she had to tell him into the background.

'What's happened?' she asked, catching some of his excitement; she just knew it was something good.

'I've just seen Jud,' Rupert replied, and unable to keep his news to himself any longer, went on joyfully, 'Jud says I've already proved I'm up to the work—he says I can have the job permanently.'

'Oh, Rupe, that's marvellous!' Lucy's own troubles were forgotten as she returned her brother's delighted grin. 'You must have done really well—your three months' trial isn't up yet, is it?'

'No, that's the great thing about it—I've been working for Jud now for two months and thought I was going to have to sweat it out for another month before he gave me his verdict. I had to go up to the Hall for something and Jud was there—he's just come back from abroad and is having a few days at home—anyway, he asked me to go with him to his study. I don't mind telling you, Lucy, I was scared stiff he was going to part company with me for all I know I've been doing a good job, but he'd got that look on his face that gives nothing away—you know, all cold with nothing of his thoughts showing.' Lucy nodded; she'd seen that look too often. 'Anyway, when he told me—I just stood there stupidly too dazed to take it in, then Jud said, "Off you go, then, young Carey, I expect you'll want to tell your sister your news".'

'He mentioned me?' Lucy hadn't meant to enquire, it was just begging for crumbs and she knew it, and she could have bitten her tongue for voicing the question; it confirmed she had made the right decision in making up her mind to leave, she had just proved that—she wasn't the type to beg from anybody.

'Oh, Jud often asks how you are,' Rupert answered offhandedly, his thoughts still on a high plateau, letting her know it would be some time before he came down again.

Lucy put her own thoughts to one side. Rupert had been through a bad time one way or another, it was only right he should live through every moment of his present jubilation.

'You'll be going out to celebrate tonight,' she said, thinking this occasion couldn't be let pass without commemorating it in some way.

'Might go down to the local later—I've got some estimates for repairs to Blue Bell farm I want to look through first. Mustn't fall down on the job as soon as I've got it.' His tone told her there was no way he was going to fall down on the job come what may.

Rupert disappeared into the study after they had had their evening meal. He had come down to earth a little by that time, and Lucy decided as she was washing up the dinner things that she would have a word with him about moving to Garbury before he went down to the pub. She was anxious to get in touch with Aunt Dorothy and get it all fixed up, but wanted to tell Rupert first. Accordingly, when he emerged from the study about an hour later, still in a happy frame of mind but having lost some of his earlier exuberance, Lucy told him what she had in mind.

'I thought you liked living here,' he said.

'Oh, I do, Rupe,' Lucy told him. 'But I feel I'd like to do a job of some sort and there's only agriculture around here —there'll be a wider scope for me near to a big city and I shall enjoy living with Aunt Dorothy.'

Rupert seemed to accept what she was saying without too much trouble, for all it was inconceivable in his view that anyone would want to live anywhere but in Priors Channing, though he did say, 'I'm going to miss you around the place, Lucy. I never did thank you for bearing with me when . . .'

'Oh, forget that,' Lucy said impulsively. 'My big worry

is how you're going to cope without someone here to see to your meals, your laundry—that sort of thing.'

Rupert went off to the pub having told her not to worry on that score; what with the salary he was earning now secure, and his quarterly allowance, he thought he could stretch to employing a housekeeper. He said he was only going out for a 'quick one', and true to his word he was back in under an hour.

'You weren't long,' Lucy said when he came in.

'I was blown back all the way—it's howling a gale out there.'

'Want anything to eat?' Lucy enquired, thinking if he didn't she would make tracks for bed.

'No, thanks—I'm still full up from your steamed pudding.'

Lucy smiled at him; he had helped himself to a second helping without waiting to be asked. 'In that case I think I'll go up.'

Lucy wasn't sleeping very well, and woke up in the middle of the night to hear thunder and see forks of lightning cracking the sky. She quite liked the rain and lay listening to it flail against the window pane, musing that if ever she lost her hearing that would be one of the sounds she would miss most.

Rupert was up and dressed when she came downstairs the next morning, and she wondered if his excitement of the night before had prevented him from sleeping. He didn't hang about in the mornings these days, but seeing him shrugging into his oilskins and wellingtons, for although the thunder and lightning had ceased it was still tipping it down outside, forced Lucy to exclaim:

'Hey, what about your breakfast?'

'No time, love—Jackson from Lower Farm was on the phone while you were still in the land of nod. The wind and rain have caused havoc to the farm and outbuildings, I shall have to go and have a look.'

Lucy privately thought Lower Farm wouldn't fall to pieces while Rupert had a spot of breakfast, but she went into the kitchen secretly applauding Rupert's keenness for his job. She thought she had said 'Cheerio' to her brother, but the back door opened after a very few minutes and he put his head round the door to yell a hurried, 'There's an envelope on the desk in the study, Jud's waiting for it. Be a pal and take it up to the Hall for me,' and before Lucy had time to form a reply, the back door was slammed shut and Rupert had gone.

Lucy's spurt of anger against her brother didn't last very long, though for a brief while she was furious—mainly, she reasoned, because the last thing she wanted to do was to go to the Hall. Then as she simmered down she realised, unwilling to go as she was, with Rupert so keen not to fall down on his job there was nothing for it but that she would have to deliver the envelope for him.

Still she wasn't in any hurry. Rupert had said Jud was home for a few days, so if she left going until after ten, by that time Jud would probably be firmly entrenched in his study and wouldn't want to be disturbed—she could hand over the envelope to Mrs Weston to give to him without ever having to see him.

She had already started on the housework when at nine o'clock Mrs Turton arrived, causing Lucy to look at her in quick apology as the woman vigorously shook out her umbrella at the back door and came into the warm kitchen.

'I'd forgotten it was your day, Mrs Turton—I'm sorry, I should have come and picked you up and saved you having to make your way through this rain.'

Mrs Turton gave her a gappy-toothed smile, accepting her apology, and proceeded to change her coat and wellingtons for an overall and slippers. 'Not fit for man nor beast this weather,' she grumbled. 'Though I expect there's some that'll say it's good for the garden—though the only thing that'll be growing if this keeps up will be rice.'

Lucy had to smile at her. For all Mrs Turton grumbled often, there was a lot of humour in her. 'I'm going out myself later,' she said, 'but I'll wait until it stops a bit first.'

'It's not going to stop,' Mrs Turton forecast, already going to the cupboard where the cleaning materials were kept. 'It'll be like this for the rest of the day.'

The rain hadn't slackened off as Mrs Turton had predicted it wouldn't by the time Lucy was ready to go out. Lucy had no mind to her appearance, sure she wouldn't be seeing Jud, and topped her jeans and sweater with her bright red shining mac and braved the elements to dash to her car.

She tried not to think as she headed the Mini in the direction of the Hall, but she had to own she felt nervous for all she was certain she wouldn't be seeing Jud.

Reaching the Hall, anxious to drop the envelope into Mrs Weston's hands and be away again, Lucy was glad it was pouring with rain, since it gave her a good excuse to dive from her car and race up the steps to the front door where she waited for her knock to be answered.

As she had hoped, Mrs Weston opened the door and Lucy was just explaining her errand, had pressed the envelope into Mrs Weston's hands and was preparing to make her getaway when a female voice calling her name halted her.

'Ah, Lucy, I thought it was you.' Lucy's heart dropped to the bottom of her shoes. Jud's mother was here! She didn't need Mrs Hemming's, 'Come in, do,' to know the flying visit she had thought to make had come unstuck, for she just couldn't be rude to her no matter what happened. She stepped over the threshold, hearing Mrs Hemming say she had been in the drawing room and had seen a streak of red flash by and had recognised the Mini from when Rupert had used it one day.

Mrs Weston took care of Lucy's mac, and Lucy, wishing now that she had changed out of her jeans, went with Mrs

Hemming into the drawing room.

'Rupert asked me to bring an envelope J-Jud is waiting for,' Lucy explained, wishing she had been able to bring out Jud's name without stammering over it. 'Rupert had to go over to Lower Farm first thing,' she added.

'That would be the farm Mr Jackson tenants?' Mrs Hemming enquired, while inviting Lucy to sit down.

Lucy agreed that it was, and added, 'I won't stay, Mrs Hemming—you weren't expecting company, and I only popped over with ...'

'Nonsense,' Mrs Hemming said firmly, for all her eyes were kind. 'You know I like to see you any time,' and then with a smile Lucy was too weak to argue against, 'You'll stay and have coffee with me, won't you?'

There was nothing Lucy could do but agree. So far she had no idea where Jud was, he might not even be in the house, but if as she had first thought he would be in his study by now, it wouldn't take her many minutes to drink her coffee and be away. She could still do it without having to see him.

'I'll just go and ask Mrs Weston to bring some coffee,' Mrs Hemming told her, moving towards the door. 'I won't be long.'

Lucy stood up as soon as the door closed behind Mrs Hemming, her anxiety to be gone too much to be taken sitting down. Why couldn't she have just pushed the envelope through the mail box at the side of the door? She heard voices in the hall and turned round expecting Mrs Hemming to come through the door, thinking she had bumped into Mrs Weston and was now asking her to bring the coffee in when it was ready.

But the smile she had on her lips for Mrs Hemming froze, then disappeared, when she saw it was not Mrs Hemming who came in, but Jud. A Jud who had that stern look on his face for all he greeted her pleasantly enough.

'Hello, Lucy.'

'I brought an envelope from Rupert,' she said, her words coming out in a hurry, so conscious was she of her love for him. She didn't want him to think she had come with a view to seeing him in mind.

'I know,' he said quietly.

So Mrs Weston had already handed it over. She would have thought Jud would have stayed in his study—if he had thought to reward her with coffee, he would know his mother would see to that.

'Rupert had to go over to Lower Farm,' she said, more slowly this time, though she felt her disquiet growing when Jud accepted this piece of information without comment, and searched round for something else to say. 'Your mother has gone to see about coffee,' she told him, wanting to add that she had changed her mind about wanting any, but not wanting him to guess at the panic that was threatening to overtake her. She loved him so much and he didn't care a damn. He looked so much in control standing there in his light slacks and sweater with his grey-green eyes piercing through her—it wasn't fair that he should be so much in control when she felt she was rapidly going to pieces.

'Won't you sit down, Lucy?' Jud invited, and as she took the chair he indicated to her, the words making her nerve ends jangle worse than ever, 'I've just seen my mother—I hope you don't mind, but I've asked her to delay the coffee for a while.'

'Delay . . .' Lucy repeated, her brain seizing up, nothing more clever coming through.

'Yes,' Jud confirmed. 'You see, Lucy, I rather wanted to have a talk with you.'

'Oh,' she said guardedly. Whatever he had to say to her could not be about Rupert, because Rupert already had the knowledge that his future was secure. If Jud had anything to say to her that concerned her personally, and though she had no idea what it could possibly be, she knew she didn't want to hear it. 'Rupert tells me you've agreed to take him on permanently,' she said brightly. 'He ... he'll do a good job for you, Jud.'

'I'm sure of it,' Jud replied, taking the seat opposite her, his face expressionless. 'I can't fault his work,' he said, and Lucy had the oddest feeling that he knew how on edge she was and was just going along with her until she felt calmer. 'He has made mistakes in the past, but ...'

'Mistakes?' Lucy queried, thinking Rupert might have put a foot wrong when he had first come to work for Jud.

'I would have said he was in error when he sold me a piece of your property without your knowledge, wouldn't you?'

She had been mistaken in thinking Jud knew how she was feeling, she realised, and felt relief at that thought, though she wished he hadn't gone straight into a discussion about something she didn't want to talk about—her mother's ring had been the start of it all ...

'Did Rupert tell you he'd asked me to sell him back the ring when he gets his money from the sale of Brook House?'

'N-no,' Lucy replied, startled, a warm feeling flooding through her at Rupert's thought. Then, her tongue coming out to lick suddenly dry lips before she asked her question, 'And did you agree to sell it back to him?' She tried to put just the right note of query into her voice, but a husky note merged with the aloof tone she had been aiming for.

'No, Lucy—I told your brother I had no intention of selling it.'

Lucy refused to say the 'Oh' that sprang to her lips, though it was a near thing. 'It's yours to do with what you wish,' she managed instead.

'Exactly, Lucy—I offered it to you with no strings attached once, do you remember?'

Would she ever forget, even now so many weeks afterwards what had followed was as vivid in her memory now as it had been then. 'Yes, I remember,' she said, amazed

that she could sound so cool when she was shaking inside.
She knew her face was growing pink and hated that he
should know she was not feeling as cool as she sounded.

'My offer is still open, Lucy,' Jud said, his eyes, having
seen her blush, refusing to leave her face.

'You mean ...'

'I mean I would like you to have your ring, and I don't
want payment for it from your brother.' He paused, then
added deliberately, 'Or, Lucy, from you.'

The fact that Jud was now telling her as if he was saying it outright that he didn't fancy her had her pride coming to her aid. 'I apologise for doubting your motives that
last time you offered to give me the ring,' she said, holding
his eyes for the briefest of seconds before looking away
again. 'I know now you want nothing from me in return,
but I'm afraid I can't accept your offer.' And then because
he was hurting her more than he knew by the cold way he
sat opposite her, letting her know that the ring she valued
so much, the money he had paid for it, meant nothing to
him—as little, she faced it squarely, as she meant to him—
and the only way she could keep her terrible hurt from
showing was by resorting to sarcasm.

'I don't doubt there's someone somewhere who'll be
pleased to pay for such an item in a way I couldn't bring
myself to.' That was it, she'd managed just the right tone.
She felt sure he couldn't avoid thinking now that if he
didn't fancy her, he could be certain he was the last man in
the world she would look at. She dared a hasty look at him
for proof that he had understood her meaning, though he
would have to be blind not to see it, she thought. She saw
his jaw was clenched, and that he was looking back at her
through narrowed eyes. She knew he didn't like what he
had heard, but who did he think he was, to think he could
say what he liked to her and get away with it? She thought
he looked as though he was struggling to keep his temper,
and though she knew the force of his rage was something

to be reckoned with, she didn't think she would come to very much harm while his mother was in the house.

'If you won't accept your ring back, Lucy, I can assure you I'll give it to no one else.' Jud's tone was harsh, confirming that his temper was pretty near to the surface.

'You think it's tainted now that I've worn it?' she jibed, hating to believe it, but hurt to her very soul, her pride refused to let him see he was ruthlessly cutting her heart out.

She was completely unprepared for Jud's reaction to her jibe. In a movement so swift she didn't see him coming he was out of his chair and hauling her to her feet, his hands gripping her shoulders in a racking hold as though he was using her to try to hang on to the last remnants of the control he had over his temper.

'By God, Lucy Carey, you try me to the very limits!' he thundered, then while she was still looking at him with startled eyes, he pulled her roughly into his arms and brought his mouth down on hers in a kiss that was as brutal as it was passionate.

Responding to his kiss was out of the question. There was nothing persuasive about the hold he had on her, it was the grip of a man who had been brought to the end of his patience and was now mindless of any hurt he inflicted. Lucy struggled against him, her heart pounding with fear as he dragged the neck of her sweater away from her and his lips ravaged the column of her throat and neck. Pushing at him was useless and kicking at him brought her so off balance it provided Jud with the excuse he didn't need to hold her even closer.

'Let me go!' she yelled at him when she found her mouth free again and the breath to speak. 'Let me go, Jud, you swine!'

'Like hell,' he grated. 'You think you can say what the hell you like and get away with it, don't you—but there's a limit, my little virgin, and I've just reached mine,' and again he swooped on her mouth.

Oh God, she was scared! Jud must have told his mother he would let her know when to come in, and Lucy guessed Mrs Hemming would think they were having a heart-to-heart talk and wouldn't interrupt them. She had dreamed of being kissed by Jud, of being held by him, but never like this. 'Please, Jud,' she cried, 'you're hurting me!' He was. She knew she would find bruises in a day or two's time, but it was the mental hurt he was inflicting that was the greater pain. The thought that when she had left Priors Channing, the memory of her last meeting with Jud would be that he was so uncaring of her he could treat her so.

Jud's hold on her held firm, and she knew he was going to ignore her pleas, then suddenly his body stilled, and with a cry that was half a groan he slackened his hold on her and he buried his face in her neck.

The groan Lucy heard sounded for all the world so full of remorse that all fear left her and knowing, with Jud's arms only loosely about her now, that escape would have been easy, she just couldn't find it in her to tear herself out of his arms to flee and leave him. The hands that seconds earlier had been pummelling at his back in an endeavour to effect her release now closed about him, and she held him as he held her, and again Jud's body stiffened and he lifted his head to look down into the wide brown eyes that showed not fear now, but gentle regret that they would always be enemies.

'Gentle Lucy,' seemed to be dragged from him. 'You always were too soft for your own good,' and with that he lowered his head once more, only this time there was none of the rage or anger in his kiss, and at that first gentle touch Lucy knew she was lost. This was so much more what she wanted, her bruised lips parted, the hands at his back clenched once, then gave in and splayed against him, drawing him to her as he was drawing her.

Mindlessly she returned his kiss, made no objection this time when her sweater was pulled away from her throat and his lips traced healing kisses where his lips had scorched before, then his mouth claimed hers once more, urgently, transmitting the same yearning urgency to her. She felt his hands at her waist, felt their warmth against her skin beneath her sweater, and her lips clung to his when his hands caressed in delicious movements to come to rest just beneath her breasts. Her breath seemed to halt as she waited, wanted his hands to continue on upwards, but it seemed as though Jud was awaiting her permission now to invade further the privacy of her body, and without thought her lips came fractionally away from his to murmur in an agony of waiting, 'Please, Jud,' in invitation for him to do with her what he would. A sigh of bliss escaped her when she felt his hands against her breasts and she pressed to him, wanting this moment to never end.

She was in complete agreement when he picked her up and carried her to the settee, and looking into his eyes she saw nothing of the coldness she remembered there, but a flame that was more green than grey, before she buried her head against him and felt his body taut beside her as the cushions moulded to their bodies.

Having invited Jud's caresses Lucy thought she was prepared to go wherever their delight took them, but when she felt the looseness of the jeans she was wearing and realised her zip must be undone, for all she hadn't felt Jud undoing it, her breath caught in her throat as choking realisation hit her when his hand began fondling movements around her navel, that now was the time to stop or ...

Her move to roll off the settee was instinctive, and once her body was away from him, cold, cruel sanity fought in her brain to be heard against the voice within her that insisted she return to Jud on the settee.

Harsh sanity won, and with hands that were shaking the three-inch gap in her jeans was fastened with a jerky movement as she pulled up the zip. She had her back to Jud and didn't dare turn round as logic she didn't want to listen to was hammering to be heard. Jud must be laughing his head off—Jud with all his experience had found the seduction of Lucy Carey child's play.

'There's no need to panic, Lucy,' she heard him say quietly behind her 'I wouldn't have ...'

'Wouldn't you?' she came back sharply, still not daring to turn as she straightened her sweater and looked round wildly for her bag. 'My God, it didn't look like it—child's play, wasn't it?' She knew she was going to break down any moment—oh, where was her bag—it had her car keys in it. She wanted to race out of here and now, but she would look a fine fool if she had to come back for her bag.

'You appear to have a fine opinion of me.' She heard an edge creeping into Jud's voice, but was uncaring of it.

'About as fine as the opinion you have of me,' she snapped back. Then knowing her pride lay in ruins—oh, how Jud would laugh when she was gone—she made a vain attempt to get away from him with at least some of her pride salvaged. 'Well, don't worry about it, Jud Hemming —I promise you I won't—in a week or two we shall be out of each other's hair, and if ever we think of—of what hap-happened—or what nearly happened,' she amended hastily, still not knowing quite where she was, 'then we can both sit back and have a damn good laugh.'

She jumped visibly to hear Jud's voice just over her shoulder; she hadn't heard him move from the settee. 'Nothing *nearly* happened,' he bit in her ear. 'I was in control the whole time.'

She could have hit him for that remark, though he sounded so sincere she had to believe him, but it made her furious that in her innocence she had been floundering in the joy of his touch, his lovemaking, that only when it looked as if he would trespass on part of her that was intensely personal had she come down to earth. She had scant satisfaction that Jud wasn't so much in control as he would have her believe, for instead of putting his hands on her again and turning her to face him, he ordered: 'Look at me, Lucy,' and frightened in case she was wrong and he would touch her again, Lucy turned to face him.

There was nothing about him now that remotely connected him with the lover he had been a few minutes ago. Nothing at all in his face to give her any indication of what he was feeling, thinking ...

'You've just said that shortly we'll be out of each other's hair,' Jud reminded her. 'Do I take it from that remark that you're going away for a while?'

A lot he cared! She could tell he would be clapping his hands before the exhaust smoke of her departure had evaporated. 'Not for a *while*, Jud—I'm going away permanently.'

Jud didn't ask where, he seemed to accept her statement without difficulty, and yet—and yet, Lucy thought, she could have sworn his jaw clenched momentarily as though he was controlling some inner impulse. Imagination, of course; Jud's face was as impassive as ever when she looked again. She had just imagined seeing something she wanted to see. Wanting some sign that he was not unmoved to hear that he would never see her again, she had dreamed up a fleeting picture of Jud looking not as cool as he would have her believe.

Knowing there was absolutely nothing more for them to say to each other, Lucy spied her bag about two yards from her feet tucked in against the settee where it had been all the time, only she'd been too panic-stricken to dare turn to see it. She moved a step away from Jud, ready to make her departure, feeling suddenly dead inside.

'Don't go.'

The hoarse note in Jud's voice stopped her more than any words he could have said, and she half turned back to him, not daring to look at him lest he see how completely defeated she was. She thought she knew the reason for his words, though the way he said them was unexpected.

'I have to go,' she told him flatly, her eyes downcast making an unseeing survey of the floor. 'We've just proved the biological urge you spoke of—I'm not your girl for further sex exploration.'

'Damn the biological urge,' Jud snapped violently, causing Lucy's head to come up sharply. She expected to see little warmth in his eyes, but there was a raging light there he did nothing to hide. 'I don't want you to go—sex has got nothing to do with it.'

Oh God, she thought, unable to believe Jud wanted nothing from her yet not understanding why he didn't want her to go. She had thought she was dead inside, yet all he had to do was look at her, tell her he didn't want her to go, even make it sound as if he meant it, and her heart was hammering within her. Her legs felt shaky and she had to look away from him before her brain would clear sufficiently for her to answer.

'Y-you say s-sex has nothing to do with your reason for wanting me to stay?' she queried, and looked at him again the words said.

She saw Jud hesitate. It was enough to have her determined to leave the room without saying another word, she didn't need him confirming slowly, 'Well, no. Don't misunderstand me, Lucy. Sex has its part in my reason for wanting you to stay, though I prefer to call it physical love . . .' Lucy's action of going to pick up her handbag, her intention to leave before he could persuade her otherwise obvious, stopped him before he could complete what he was saying.

She had to go, and go now. Jud could call sex by any name he chose, though she couldn't help the let-down feeling that he could resort to use the words 'physical love'— she had thought he would be more honest than that. If she stayed with him another second she knew she would be accepting whatever relationship he had in mind —but when it was over, when he had tired of her, what then? She couldn't understand the very stillness of him, though she thought it might be because Jud would never beg any woman, and having asked her once to stay, he would not ask her again. She reached the door. Jud hadn't moved, and she knew her surmise was correct, he wouldn't ask her again, but pride demanded she had the last word, for all she didn't think her pride would last very long once she got through that door.

'No, thanks, Jud. What you have in mind isn't for me,' She felt the cold round porcelain knob of the door beneath her fingers and thought there was nothing more he could say that would have her answering, but when his words hit her ears, instead of turning the door knob and making her escape, she found herself clinging on to it as though it was a lifeline giving her support.

'Marry me, Lucy.'

The voice that hit her ears had a strangled, almost despairing note to it and for a dizzying second she thought someone else had come into the room, so unlike Jud's voice did it sound. Then the world righted itself and beads of sweat broke out on her forehead, because she so wanted to marry him, but not for the reasons he was asking.

'Marry you, Jud?' she scoffed, and only she knew how much it hurt to inject that tone into her voice as tears she was unaware of shedding rolled silently down her face. 'Why? Because you can't get me any other way?'

'No, damn you!' If she was feeling hurt, Jud sounded as though what she had said as much as the way she had said it had mortally wounded him. 'I asked you to marry me because I love you.' The cold note she was familiar with had taken possession again, and if she had ever dreamed of a man she loved telling her he loved her, it had never been with those freezing tones as though he hated her, but while her control was rapidly going to pieces, Jud's control was coming to ice him over as he added cuttingly, 'I have your answer—now get out.'

When Lucy turned round he had his back to her and she knew while her heart sang and tears rained down her face that his action of turning away from her was the action of a man who suspected she might turn once before leaving and who wasn't going to let her see his pain. Oh, how she loved him—and to think he had said he loved her! She still couldn't take it in, but wanted so badly to believe it, she just had to stay in the hope he would say it again. She saw his hands were clenched tightly at his sides, and realised he was waiting to hear the sound of the door opening and closing to know she had gone before he relaxed the stern control he was exercising.

He confirmed it by grating, 'Get the hell out of here, Lucy—I won't be responsible for ...'

'I love you, Jud,' Lucy broke in as a wave of impulsive courage shot through her.

Slowly Jud turned, the sight of her tear-wet face not moving him. His face was marble-cold except for his eyes that pierced through her, telling her that if she was lying heaven help her. 'Repeat that statement,' he said, his hands still clenched, not moving.

'I ... I said—I ... love you, Jud.'

She barely got his name out when he moved and she was in his arms, the salt of her tears being blotted by his lips and face as he kissed her and hugged her to him, first laying his cheek against hers, then hungry for her lips and eagerly claiming them, then kissing her eyes.

'Oh, Lucy, Lucy girl, what a hell of a time you've given me!'

'And you me—Oh, Jud, if you knew how unhappy I've been!'

Jud's kisses drugged away all unhappiness as with broken endearments they clung to each other.

'Oh, Jud, I feel I could faint, I'm so happy,' Lucy confessed at last.

'Believe it or not, my knees aren't feeling all that strong

either,' Jud told her, for all she didn't believe him, though he did guide her to the settee where they sat down, and with his arm around her, her head against his chest, though she did have to keep lifting her head every now and then to look at him to make sure it was really Jud who held her, she asked him why he had never given her the smallest sign he cared.

'I was afraid to,' said the man Lucy had thought was afraid of nothing. She raised her head questioningly. 'It's true,' Jud told her, reading her look. 'The first time I saw you I desired you.' Lucy remembered the look she thought she had seen that morning at the village hall. 'I thought I'd caught your eye—thought, I must admit,' he confessed, 'that you knew the rules, but when I went to follow through you'd looked away and I realised you weren't playing.'

'We hadn't even been introduced,' Lucy protested, and a light laugh broke from Jud, because they both knew it would have made no difference with or without an introduction.

Jud hugged her to him and continued, 'You're beautiful, Lucy, but at that time I thought I knew of several other women who could match your beauty, but I was conscious of you the whole time, and when you chose to look through me—well, to tell the truth, it was a pretty new experience for me and, if you'll forgive me saying so, I made up my mind to have you.'

Lucy blushed and Jud's arm tightened about her. 'You didn't look as if you'd even seen me,' she said softly. 'I remember thinking I'd read that first look—I ... I'd seen it before, but ...'

'But affairs weren't in your line—I learned that very quickly,' Jud said, giving her a chaste kiss before going on. 'I found out who you were, thought then you must know I was the man who had bought the ring from Rupert and—I'm sorry, darling, but I thought you were peeved because you hadn't wanted him to sell it.'

Lucy latched on to his line of thinking. 'You thought I was some gold-digging harpy and that I objected to Rupert selling what you thought was his because I wanted it?'

'Yes, I did,' Jud told her. 'But I was still determined to get to know you. I had my mother and Carol staying with me at the time, but even so I would have contacted you the next day under some pretext or other. Then wham, there you were at my front door without me having to move a muscle.'

'You were so cold, so unfeeling,' Lucy told him, and was held close and kissed almost senseless for a few minutes.

'Any complaints?' Jud teased, and she knew he was trying to get them both on an even keel before things got out of hand.

'None,' she said huskily, then with a teasing note of her own, 'My first—no, second impression of you has undergone a drastic change.'

'As mine did of you,' Jud told her gently. 'Inside a very few moments I knew you were a woman totally outside my experience. I had to make sure we would have a point of contact, so I wasted no time in getting engaged to you.'

'But that was to try and get Carol to fall out of love with you, wasn't it?'

Jud laughed quietly as he denied it. 'A ruse, my love,' he told her. 'Carol is fond of me, but only in a sisterly way. Your thinking she was my fiancée gave me the ideal opportunity to keep you believing she was in love with me and so invent a reason for you and me to be engaged.'

'But Carol said, that day at the village hall, that she hoped to live here.'

'She did?' Jud queried, and Lucy went on to explain about Carol crossing her fingers when she had said she didn't come from Priors Channing.

Jud grinned when Lucy had finished. 'That's Carol,' he said. 'She can be a bit of a pest at times, and I can only imagine that since prior to my meeting a certain dark-eyed, beautiful Lucy Carey, I was a confirmed bachelor, Carol not knowing you—you could have been the village chatterbox for all she knew—let you believe she was hoping to move into the Hall to stimulate village gossip. Actually Carol did me a favour, because after you'd gone the night we became engaged I told her to be a sport and disappear for three months.'

'You didn't?' Lucy challenged, though believing him. 'And she went just like that?'

'Well, not without wanting to know why, but since she'd got fish of her own to fry, namely some young man lounging around in Tenerife, she didn't press too hard to find out.'

They were silent for some moments, Lucy being heartily glad Carol wasn't in love with Jud. She had liked the girl from the start and was looking forward to getting to know her.

'When did you know you loved me?' she asked. 'I didn't know I loved you until I came here to return your ring.'

Jud remembered the occasion and his arms tightened hard about her. 'I've got a pig of a temper, haven't I?' he said regretfully. 'But believe it or not, just lately the only person who's made me lose control of it has been you. You intrigued me from the start, but it wasn't until you had gone that night that I stopped to think why was it I had so little control of my temper when you were around—that same night I knew I was in love with you. I wanted to come over to Brook House as soon as I knew and insist that you keep the ring, but I felt so sick with the way I'd frightened you half to death I had to hold back. Then when I did come to see you we seemed to bring out the worst in each other.' Lucy recalled that dreadful slap she had served him with, and her arms gripped tightly round his waist. 'Well, after that I could see we both needed a cooling off period, so I

decided to keep away from you for as long as I could—
but after six weeks I'd had it, and knowing you would refuse any invitation I issued, I arranged a dinner party making sure you would be there.'

'You mean that bit about Rupert letting the side down
was all made up ...'

'Forgive me?' Jud asked, and knew himself forgiven
when Lucy reached up and kissed him. 'That evening didn't
end up as I had planned either,' he went on. 'Then I had
to go abroad on business, with my mind never less on business, I can tell you—every day I wanted to telephone you,
wanted to hear your voice, and it was then I decided I'd
had it. I had to have something settled one way or the
other. I was going to come over and see you this afternoon.'

'But I came here instead.'

'And I'm so glad you did, my darling.'

They were content in each other's arms for a while, then
Lucy said softly, 'And all this started from my mother's
ring ...'

'That ring has caused more trouble than enough between
us, sweetheart,' said Jud, kissing her gently, then putting
his hand into his trouser pocket withdrew the square box
she knew so well. 'Will you accept it now, Lucy, with my
love?'

Lucy felt tears spurt to the back of her eyes. 'Are—are
we engaged?' she asked uncertainly.

'I'm going to marry you, Lucy,' Jud told her, his face
serious, then with a touch of aggression, 'You're not thinking of backing out, are you?'

'Oh no, Jud—I love you.'

'Good,' said Jud, promptly kissing her. 'In that case,
Lucy my darling, we definitely *are* engaged—though if you
wouldn't mind I would like us both to choose the ring
you're to wear as mine—your mother's ring I return to
you.'

'Oh, Jud,' Lucy said helplessly. Then looking at him with

all the love she felt for him showing in her beautiful face, 'Will you give me this ring on our wedding day?'

Jud looked back at her, his face showing warmth, love and understanding. His Lucy was no gold-digger. 'You won't have long to wait, my dearest love,' he told her.

YOUR 1980 ROMANCE HOROSCOPE!

Harlequin Reader Service

In U.S.A.
M.P.O. Box 707
Niagara Falls, NY 14302

In Canada
649 Ontario Street
Stratford, Ontario, N5A 6W2

Please send me the following Harlequin Romance Horoscope volumes. I am enclosing a check or money order of $1.75 for each volume ordered, plus 40¢ to cover postage and handling.

☐ **Aries**
(Mar. 21-Apr. 20)

☐ **Taurus**
(Apr. 21-May 22)

☐ **Gemini**
(May 23-June 21)

☐ **Cancer**
(June 22-July 22)

☐ **Leo**
(July 23-Aug. 22)

☐ **Virgo**
(Aug. 23-Sept. 22)

☐ **Libra**
(Sept. 23-Oct. 22)

☐ **Scorpio**
(Oct. 23-Nov. 21)

☐ **Sagittarius**
(Nov. 22-Dec. 22)

☐ **Capricorn**
(Dec. 23-Jan. 20)

☐ **Aquarius**
(Jan. 21-Feb. 19)

☐ **Pisces**
(Feb. 20-Mar. 20)

Number of volumes checked @ $1.75 each	$_____
N.Y. and N.J. residents add appropriate sales tax	$_____
Postage and handling	$____.40
TOTAL:	$_____
I am enclosing a grand total of	$_____

NAME_____

ADDRESS_____

STATE/PROV._____ ZIP/POSTAL CODE_____

ROM 2302